"WHAT A

Becky turned to face the guy Dakota was full-on gawking at. Not very subtle, but subtle was her normal approach, and fulfilling Dakota's plan called for abnormal behavior.

He was standing in the doorway, giving her dirty lumberjack in a flannel and jeans that made her want to go over there and squeeze his tush. He was giving her Henry Cavill as pre-Superman pulling clothes off a washline in the rain. He was giving her all-man, all-hairy forearms and dark hair and looking strong enough to climb.

And then he was giving her a look, and those eyes shot right into her gut as he matched her ogle with a curious heat of his own.

Dang, she should come to sports bars more often.

"Quit drooling," Dakota whispered to her.

"No."

"Well then, go talk to him. Quick, before the two of you undress each other with your eyes." Dakota fanned herself. "Lucky girl, go on."

Also by Sarah Title

Kentucky Home

Kentucky Christmas

Home Sweet Home

Snowed In

Two Family Home

Practice Makes Perfect

The Undateable

Falling for Trouble

And read more Sarah Title in

Delicious

The Most Wonderful Time

Laws *of* Attraction

SARAH TITLE

ZEBRA BOOKS
KENSINGTON PUBLISHING CORP.
http://www.kensingtonbooks.com

ZEBRA BOOKS are published by

Kensington Publishing Corp.
119 West 40th Street
New York, NY 10018

All Kensington titles, imprints, and distributed lines are available at special quantity discounts for bulk purchases for sales promotion, premiums, fundraising, educational, or institutional use.

Special book excerpts or customized printings can also be created to fit specific needs. For details, write or phone the office of the Kensington Sales Manager: Attn.: Sales Department. Kensington Publishing Corp., 119 West 40th Street, New York, NY 10018. Phone: 1-800-221-2647.

Zebra and the Z logo Reg. U.S. Pat. & TM Off.

First Printing: November 2017
ISBN-13: 978-1-4201-4187-0
ISBN-10: 1-4201-4187-2

eISBN-13: 978-1-4201-4188-7
eISBN-10: 1-4201-4188-0

10 9 8 7 6 5 4 3 2 1

Printed in the United States of America

To Dana,
who showed me that fostering is perfect for
the commitment-phobic dog lover.

And for Trish,
who let me pretend I was just fostering Starr.

ACKNOWLEDGMENTS

Many, many thanks to Anne Lucke and Sarah Glassmeyer for entertaining my questions about law librarianship, and I'm terribly sorry if I didn't accurately capture the amount of smoochin' you all encounter on a daily basis. Thanks to Kelly, Brian, and everyone else who unwittingly supplied me with dog names. Also, thanks for having real cute dogs. Brock Savage, thank you for talking me through many iterations of the ending of this story. Dang, plots. Thank you forever to Alicia Condon at Kensington for believing in my stories, and to Louise Fury for playing it cool when I cannot.

And an extra special librarian thank you to folks who read and share because that fosters our community of obsessive connoisseurs of the happy ending. Plus, stories of women getting what they want, of being empowered and sexually satisfied, make people uncomfortable and scared that the secret will get out and that we will take over the world. We need each other.

Chapter One

"What about that one?"

Becky followed her best friend's not-very-subtle pointing toward a guy in a Broncos hat with his eyes glued to one of the seven big-screen TVs in the bar.

"Never mind, he's too into the sportsball," Dakota said.

"Dakota, I'm not—"

"Hush. Hey, *he's* kind of cute." She nodded toward a tall, dark-haired man in a suit who had just stepped up to the bar, loosening his tie. "The suit makes me think he's probably boring, so you'll like that."

Becky shook her head. "I thought the point was for me to have a one-night stand with someone who *isn't* my type."

"Oh yeah. Maybe I'll go talk to him. Dang."

Dakota's distraction wasn't distracting enough, unfortunately, and she continued to scan the bar for men Becky could have random sex with.

It was all a very fun game they were playing because Becky had been dumped, once again. And Dakota had a bee in her bonnet that Becky chose the wrong kind of guy to date, and then came up with the brilliant idea that they needed to reset Becky's sex drive by getting her laid by someone who was totally not her type. Which wasn't fair. Becky didn't have a type. She just wanted to settle down with a nice, normal guy like Paul, the kind of guy who had a job and a normal family and—fine, his apartment was kind of a sty and he'd just bought these really weird paisley curtains she'd laughed at and he got offended . . .

"Stop thinking about him."

"I'm not!" Becky insisted. She was thinking about his curtains.

"You're a terrible liar," Dakota said.

That was true.

"The only thing you're worse at than lying is picking boyfriends."

"There was nothing wrong with Paul." He didn't want to date her anymore, sure, but he wasn't a bad person. "Just because he's not *your* type."

"Becky," Dakota insisted, "you are way too nice. There was a lot wrong with that dude."

"Like what?"

"Uh-uh. No. We're not talking about this anymore. Tonight was supposed to be the night we doused the pain of your heartbreak."

"I'm not heartbroken!" Becky insisted. She was just . . . well, she was sad, that was all. Not the same as heartbroken. She was sad, and a little tipsy, and that was why her eyes were pricking with tears.

"Oh, Beck," Dakota said and enveloped her in a full-body hug. "He was so not worth it."

"I know!" she insisted, because she did. Paul wasn't a bad guy, but he was a crappy boyfriend. He was so crappy that he wouldn't even admit he was her boyfriend, even after six months of monogamy.

"But we're not talking about it, because if we're talking about it, you're thinking about it, and you need to stop thinking about the completely forgettable, totally-not-worth-it Paul. How about him?"

She pointed to a guy in very nicely fitted jeans who had his arm around a petite woman in similarly nice-fitting jeans.

"Um, I think he's taken."

"You don't know that! It could be his sister."

Mr. Jeans leaned down and planted a sloppy kiss on Ms. Jeans's mouth.

"Eh, fine," Dakota gracefully conceded. "Maybe it's the venue. I just thought a sports bar would be full of dudes."

"I still don't understand how it's possible you've never been to a sports bar before."

"I hate TV." That was true. Dakota was the only woman Becky knew for whom *Netflix and chill* was a deal breaker. She wouldn't even watch TV for the sake of the euphemism. "If a guy wants to have sex, he should just invite me over for sex," Dakota was fond of saying.

Becky preferred the euphemism. At least, she

thought she did. But it wasn't getting her very far in the romance department.

What Dakota didn't understand was that sports bars were full of bros, those suburban white guys who grew up with natural athletic prowess, good-enough intellect, and never had to deal with bullying or, like, actual problems. Paul was a bro. He wore rugby shirts but didn't play rugby. He still talked to all his frat brothers. He didn't understand the misogyny inherent in the system. Becky shouldn't date bros. Bros didn't usually date girls like her either—bookish girls with too much imagination and sunny dispositions that belied the huge chips on their shoulders for people who grew up having it easy. She shouldn't have dated Paul, that was for sure, because look where that got her?

Dumped, buzzed on beer, and surrounded by the kind of guy she wasn't supposed to be dating anymore.

She wasn't supposed to be dating anymore, period.

"You look glum," Dakota told her. "You don't want to sleep with the kind of guy who wants to sleep with a girl who looks glum."

"I'm not glum."

"You need more beer. It's your round."

Becky sighed and picked up her purse. The bar was three-dudes deep and she was going to have to jostle and push her way through, which was annoying.

Dakota grabbed her purse from her. "I should make you try to get someone to buy us a round."

Becky grabbed her purse back. "Baby steps."

"OK, baby steps. First, a little physical interaction. Then, sex!"

Becky widened her eyes in embarrassment, trying to channel a look that said, *I know you're my best friend, but please shut up*. It didn't work.

"Hey, a girl's gotta get her rocks off, too, you know. You should try it some time, Beck."

"I did get my rocks off."

"Don't say it—"

"With Paul."

"Girl, you barely got your rocks tumbled with that guy."

Becky immediately regretted the less-than-steamy details of her sex life that she'd spilled over the last bottle of wine they'd shared.

"You shouldn't settle for that."

"I didn't think I was settling!"

"Please. That's your problem, Beck. You don't want to get your rocks off unless it comes with a spare key and half of the closet."

"What? No! I can . . . ugh, I can't keep saying 'get my rocks off.'"

"I'm just saying, you're young—"

Becky raised an eyebrow.

"You're hot—"

Becky raised the other one.

"Now is not the time to be settling down. Now is the time to sow your wild oats!"

Dakota's enthusiasm was starting to draw the attention of other bar patrons. Only Dakota could tear a man's gaze away from a dozen sports-ball games.

"'Sow your wild oats'? Why are we talking like old-timers?"

"You durned whippersnapper, ain't you kids ever heard of casual sex?"

"Hey, I can have casual sex!"

Dakota got a determined gleam in her eye. Becky knew what was going to come out of her mouth before she even said it.

"Prove it."

Becky went for a mouthful of beer, only to find there were no mouthfuls left. Maybe Dakota would go get this round. Maybe she would go away and never come back.

"I bet you can't," Dakota goaded.

"I'm not taking a bet about casual sex!"

"Why not?"

"This is how all those romcoms start. I'll take the bet and go home with the rando and he'll be the love of my life. Except then he'll turn out to be a commitment-phobic narcissist with bad taste in curtains and I'll end up shouting over the crowds in a loud sports bar drinking beer and waking up with a hangover and what's the point?"

"I hate it when romcoms end like that."

"You know what I mean."

"I don't even think *you* know what you mean."

The truth was, Becky wanted to meet the love of her life. She wanted marriage and kids and all those boring, traditional things her feminist heart felt a little guilty about wanting. She wanted equal pay for equal work, too. She just also wanted someone to go home to at the end of the day, someone to cook dinner with and talk about how great it was to be earning the same amount of money.

Not that picking up a stranger in a bar would net her any of that.

"I'm just saying that I don't see how going home with a stranger is going to get me any closer to the love of my life."

"No. No love stuff. You're too focused on it." Dakota said, just when Becky was starting to warm to the idea of taking home a stranger who turned out to be her one true love. "You're obsessed with love and you keep trying to make it work with guys who don't deserve you. You need just pure, straight-up, no-strings-attached sex."

"I do?"

"Yes. Hot, sweaty, dirty sex with someone who makes you see stars and who you never have to see again."

That didn't sound terrible. It had been a really long time since she'd had hot, sweaty, dirty sex. Paul was more of a lights-off, man-on-top kind of guy.

"But what if I fall in love with the dirty-sex guy?"

Dakota shook her head. "No. You can't. You can't even think about that, because if you think it's a possibility, you'll start putting your eggs in his basket and, knowing your taste in men, his basket will have a hole in the bottom. Or a wife," she added, and they took a moment to remember the guy before Paul, the one who worked late hours during the week, or so he said. Turned out, he wasn't busy at work. He was busy with his wife.

"Seriously, Beck, the guy didn't even deny it,"

she said. "He was just stringing you along for his own ego. You don't deserve shit like that. No, you deserve—" Dakota made a gesture that had some of the bros looking over at them curiously.

"I don't know if I can handle that," Becky said.

"Becky Schrader! You are a liberated woman in control of your own sexuality!"

"Yes, but—"

"Beck, you could have any guy in this room and you're settling! You have marriage blinders on. You're seeing the trees of quote-unquote good matches and you're missing out on a whole forest of dazzling sexual experiences."

"A whole forest?"

"Babe, there are forests out there you haven't even imagined. Or at least haven't imagined in a while."

Becky instantly and again regretted ever sharing every detail of her sex life with her best friend. But Dakota wasn't wrong. Becky wanted a normal life, that was true. That wasn't going to change. But . . . she was bored. And maybe Dakota was right. Becky was so focused on the right way to achieve her normal life—meet, date, commit—but it wasn't working. No matter how many Pauls or Russes or Phils she met, she wasn't finding the one who would stick. Maybe she needed a break.

She could definitely do with a break from her normal life.

Oh God, she was starting to agree with Dakota.

"I can see you're starting to agree with me." Ha, so Dakota could read her looks. She just ignored them when it suited her.

Dakota handed her back her purse. "Let's discuss this over another round."

Becky rolled her eyes and started toward the bar. There was a big play—sportsball!—and a cheer went up and she almost got elbowed in the nose, but the distraction enabled her to sneak through the crowd and make eye contact with the bartender. He was cute. She'd never slept with a bartender before. But if she wanted to sleep with him, she'd have to stick around until after his shift was over, and she didn't think she could stay up that late.

Wow, was she a thrill seeker or what?

No wonder she dated boring guys like Paul. Hell, she half-expected Paul to walk into this bar at any moment. Except Paul was away for the weekend, at a cousin's wedding. To which she hadn't been invited. Because she wasn't his girlfriend.

Not that she particularly wanted to go to a family wedding, but it would have been nice to have been asked.

That first part wasn't true. She'd never been to a big family wedding before. She didn't have a big extended family; her family was . . . well, they weren't much on traditional celebrations. And Becky may have said as much to Paul when he mentioned the cousin's impending nuptials.

Hmph.

She took the beer and her change but left the bartender a nice tip because she wasn't going to have sex with him and headed back to Dakota.

Dakota, of course, was no longer alone.

She had been joined by two guys—oh, great, a setup. One was about Dakota's height, which wasn't tall, wearing a Broncos sweatshirt and a game day scarf, which Dakota was clearly pointing at and mocking. It looked like the guy thought Dakota was flirting. *Poor guy*, Becky thought. The other guy was wearing a similar sweatshirt, no scarf, and . . . a wedding ring.

Hadn't she and Dakota just talked about this?

"Here," she said, shoving the beer at her friend, who wasn't doing a good job of following through on the thing that was her stupid idea in the first place.

"Thank God," Dakota said.

Becky looked at the two guys. They smiled at her. She smiled back. She looked at Dakota. Dakota looked back at her.

"Hi, I'm Rick," said the guy with the wedding ring. Becky shook the hand he offered. "This is Eric."

"Rick and Eric?"

"Eric was just explaining to me that I should call him Bullhorn," Dakota said.

"That's what they called me in college," Eric—Bullhorn—said.

"Because nothing is more attractive to a woman in her thirties than a man who is still riding high on his college days," Dakota explained.

"It's because I'm so loud," Bullhorn explained. He didn't seem that loud to Becky. She could hear him over the crowd, but his voice didn't seem that nickname worthy.

"We're just borrowing some table space," Rick explained. "We don't want to interrupt." He elbowed Bullhorn, who ignored him. He seemed nice, this Rick. Too bad he was married.

"See, now, this is the kind of guy you need to avoid," Dakota said, pointing at Rick. Rick looked alarmed.

"Oh, I wasn't . . . I mean . . . I don't . . ." He held up his left hand. "I'm not trying anything here. Really, we just wanted a place to stand."

"It doesn't matter. Even if you were trying something, you are no longer Becky's type."

"What about your type?" Bullhorn asked Dakota.

"My type is short guys with unfortunate nicknames."

Rather than being deflated by Dakota's withering sarcasm, Bullhorn puffed out his chest. "Perfect!"

Dakota rolled her eyes—this guy was going to give her a headache with all the eye rolls he was causing—and turned back to scanning the crowd. Becky gave both the guys a small smile and followed Dakota's investigation.

After a minute or two, Rick and Bullhorn started talking to each other, and they didn't pay any attention as Dakota pointed out a guy in a red toboggan (too loud), another guy in a suit (whoops, forgot about the no-suits thing), and a guy in a very tight T-shirt (too in love with his own muscles).

"I have a great idea," Becky said. "How about if we just finish these beers and go somewhere else?"

Dakota sighed. "Fine. At least I never have to go to a sports bar again. Wait—" She stopped and grabbed Becky's wrist. "What about him?"

Becky turned to face the guy Dakota was full-on gawking at. Not very subtle, but subtle was her normal approach, and fulfilling Dakota's plan called for abnormal behavior.

He was standing in the doorway, giving her dirty lumberjack in a flannel and jeans that made her want to go over there and squeeze his tush. He was giving her Henry Cavill as pre-Superman pulling clothes off a washline in the rain. He was giving her all-man, all-hairy forearms and dark hair and looking strong enough to climb.

And then he was giving her a look, and those eyes shot right into her gut as he matched her ogle with a curious heat of his own.

Dang, she should come to sports bars more often.

"Quit drooling," Dakota whispered to her.

"No."

"Well, then, go talk to him. Quick, before the two of you undress each other with your eyes." Dakota fanned herself. "Lucky girl, go on." She nudged Becky with her hip, and Becky was going to do it, she was actually going to approach a guy and straight-up proposition him for hot, lumberjack sex.

Then they learned how Bullhorn earned his nickname.

Because he shouted, "Deke the Freak!" and called the guy over.

* * *

Foster Deacon was experiencing decidedly mixed feelings as he entered the bar where he was meeting his old frat brothers to watch the game. On the one hand, it would be good to see them. He hadn't kept up with them at all when he moved to New York after law school, and besides, he had planned on watching the game anyway. On the other hand, he really didn't have the mental energy to be out in public. He had too much unpacking to do. He barely had time to shower, and he definitely hadn't had the time—or energy—to shave. And he'd had to turn down an invitation from Madison to hang out, and wasn't that part of the point of moving back to Denver? Temporarily? Temporarily moving back.

He had mixed feelings about that, too.

Not about Denver. He loved Denver, even if she did kick his ass with an altitude sickness hangover on his first night back. But his family was here, and his mom would take his move—temporary move—as an indication he was ready to settle down, which he was not. He was just here to win a big case for a law firm that wasn't run by his father and to do whatever he could to keep his baby sister out of trouble.

Once that was done, he was out of here.

"Deke the Freak!"

It didn't take him long to find Rick and Eric in the crowd. Rick was almost seven feet tall, and even if he wasn't, well, Eric hadn't earned the nickname Bullhorn for nothing.

"Just like old times, man," Rick said as Foster got close enough to hear without Rick yelling. And it was. How many sports bars had they gone to, surrounded by folks cheering for the Broncos or the Rockies, with the occasional table of pretty girls thrown in? As he and Rick did the handshake into one-armed man hug, Foster got a better look at the woman he'd locked eyes with at the entrance. But she was having a whispered conversation with her friend, which was just as well. Foster was here to catch up with his friends, not to settle down.

Not that he would necessarily have to settle down with her.

"Just in time, brother. It's your round," Bullhorn said, giving him a lightish shove toward the bar.

Just like old times.

Well, if he was going to the bar . . .

"Can I get you guys anything?" he asked their tablemates. Just to be friendly. He might be tired, but he was still a gentleman.

The one who'd caught his eye earlier—the blonde one—looked surprised. But why should she be surprised? Hot girl, good manners = buy a drink.

"No, thanks," she said, holding up her still very-full pint of beer. "I've got—"

"She'd love it," her friend said, nudging the blonde. "That's very nice, thank you."

"Thank you," the blonde parroted.

By the time he got back to the table with a bucket of beers—easier to carry than five pints—Bullhorn was regaling them with a story that had them riveted.

"And that's how he got the name Deke the Freak."

Well, there went any chance of sharing his sweet time in Colorado with the hot blonde.

He never should have let Bullhorn talk him into amateur night at that dance club. Foster was a terrible dancer. And too drunk to realize that taking his shirt off had not made him a better one. And that taking off one's jeans surrounded by screaming drunk people while also drunk was not a graceful way to end his first and last night on the stage. When it got really cold, he still had an ache in his hip.

"That was ten years ago," Foster reminded him as both women looked at him with renewed interest. Mostly laughing interest, but, well, that was what he got for trying to have a reunion with Bullhorn.

"Cancuuuuuuuuuuuun!" Bullhorn was howling as Rick approached with a round of shots. When had Rick gotten a round of shots?

"As soon as he started telling that story, I figured you'd need this," he said, handing Foster some liquid salvation. Rick offered them around, and Foster noticed the blonde didn't take one, but she gamely cheered with her beer. Foster downed the shot and let it burn all the way down. God, that hurt.

"Welcome back, Deke." Rick wasn't quite as shouty as Eric was, but he seemed to be on the verge of getting sentimental. "The crew is back together."

"The crew!" Bullhorn shouted, and the two of them did the whole grunt-grunt-grunt-woo! thing they used to do that had gotten them kicked out of many sports bars like this one.

"So, you're not from around here?" the blonde asked. OK, good. They were talking.

"I am," he said as a touchdown shout went up from the crowd. He leaned in so she could hear him. "I am. But I just moved back. Just temporarily."

"Oh, that's great!" she said, with more enthusiasm than he thought the comment really warranted. But, well, she looked cute when she was enthusiastic.

"How about you? Are you from around here?"

"Born and raised."

He didn't want to get into the whole what-school-did-you-go-to thing; he went to a private boys' school, so the chances she was a fellow alum were pretty slim. In fact, he didn't want to get into any boring stuff from the past. He was here to look forward. To make partner and to move on.

"I'm Becky," she said, and stuck out her hand.

And that was what electricity felt like.

She looked surprised and pulled her hand back, but she didn't break eye contact. She tucked her hair behind her ear and bit her lip, but she didn't break eye contact.

He lost count of the rounds they ordered, although he didn't have more than one beer after that shot. Becky seemed to be nursing that one pint as well. She was a slow drinker. She was also funny and self-deprecating and really seemed to like his beard, if the amount of time she spent glancing at it was any indication.

Foster was very glad he'd had neither the time nor the energy to shave.

He was also glad he hadn't given in to the urge to unpack, no matter how much he hated the idea of living out of a suitcase for a minute longer.

He liked talking to Becky. He wouldn't mind talking to her again. Maybe walking her to her car. Getting her number. Seeing if she wanted to go in for a kiss . . .

"Deke, we're gonna go hit up Pete's," Rick said to him. "You comin'?"

Well, it hadn't been much of a reunion because he'd barely spoken to Rick—just enough to learn that the wife and kids were doing fine—and couldn't get a word in edgewise with Bullhorn.

"Breakfast burrito with chili," Bullhorn shouted.

He wasn't drunk enough to find Pete's greasy food appealing—he'd never even been to Pete's Kitchen sober—but he felt like he should make an effort to have an actual conversation with his friends.

But then there was Becky, fiddling with the ends of her hair and taking those not-very-subtle glances at his beard.

Eh, they were guys. They didn't need conversation.

"Um, you know what?" Foster said. "I think I'm gonna stick around here. Watch the end of the game."

"You mean the game that ended ten minutes ago?" Rick elbowed Bullhorn.

"Oh, got it. Catch ya later, dude."

"Dude?" Becky's friend asked, pulling on her coat. "What are you, a Colorado surfer?"

"Catch a wave, brah," Bullhorn said, flashing a hang-loose sign.

"Wait, are you going?" Becky asked her friend.

"Yeah. Gosh, I'm so tired. Gotta get up early in the morning."

Becky arched her eyebrow. Her friend fake yawned.

"But listen, you don't have to leave on my account. Deke will walk you to your car."

"I will," Foster volunteered. "If you want to stay."

"Sure. Sure, I'll stay."

"May I treat you to an omelet, m'lady?" Bullhorn asked Becky's friend.

"Do they have vegan omelets?"

"What do you think this is, Boulder?"

"And you're not vegan," Becky said, looking a little confused.

"I know. Come on, Bullhorn. Buy me some breakfast." She took his arm and led him out the door. Foster wasn't sure if he'd ever seen Bullhorn so happy.

Rick waved at them and followed the new couple out the door.

"Well." Becky swirled the little left in her glass. "Your friends are nice."

"So is yours."

"She is. I'm a little nervous she's going to eat Bullhorn alive."

"Probably. But he'll love every minute of it."

"He will?"

"Bullhorn's always had a thing for bossy women."

"Hey, Dakota's not bossy." She pursed her lips at him like she was annoyed. Then she unpursed them. "Actually, yes, she is. Hey, let's not talk about Dakota."

"Or Bullhorn."

"Or the fact that you have a friend named Bull-horn."

He laughed. Then a silence settled over them. He wasn't sure if it was awkward exactly. But it felt like an impatient silence. Maybe that was just him. He knew what he wanted, but he didn't want to be the one to bring it up. He was a gentleman, after all.

"So . . . uh. Have you read any good books lately?"

And that was what he was waiting for. For her to bring up reading.

He smiled, because it was a sweet question, and if she wasn't as ready to jump into his pants as he was into hers, he wasn't going to push it.

Chapter Two

As Deke started describing the book he'd started on the flight to Denver—the one with *The Girl* in the title that was subverting all those damsel-in-distress genre conventions—Becky did her very best to resist the urge to jump down his pants.

She thought he was putting out signals. He kept looking at her lips. He was laughing at her bad jokes. He had his hand resting on the back of her barstool.

He was the lumberjack of her dreams. All she had to do was make the first move.

"I loved that book," she said and put a hand on his wrist, the one that was still on the table.

"Don't spoil the ending," he warned, shifting a little and intertwining his fingers with hers.

"Oh, so I shouldn't tell you that it was the ghost of the hero's possessive mother?"

"Wow, that's a twist. As long as the dog doesn't die at the end. I can't deal with a book where the dog dies in the end."

Oh God. She was in love.

She leaned in and whispered the most erotic thing she could think of in this emptying sports bar to a virtual stranger. "The dog doesn't die at the end."

He shivered.

She might have nipped his earlobe.

He cursed.

"Do you want to walk me to my car?" she asked, toying with the sleeve of his shirt. Who was this woman? Who was this sexpot Becky, seducing sexy lumberjacks? Maybe Dakota was right. Maybe this was the reset she needed.

"Not really."

Oh.

"But I live not too far from here, if you want to come up for a drink. A coffee. A water. I might have some orange juice."

"That's quite a menu."

"I'm trying to be enticing."

"I'm pretty sure you don't need a full bar for that." Oh my God, she was totally flirting!

And it was working!

Because he leaned in, and those lips she'd been staring at all night were right there, on hers, and she squeezed his forearm—holy crap, that forearm—until he moved it and cupped her cheek.

As far as kisses went, it wasn't the kind of deep, passionate, all-consuming kiss she'd been imagining ever since he and those lips had walked into the bar, but it was hot, and it held the promise of more to come.

"Not far?"

"Not far."

She smiled. She was so ready for a reset.

He did live conveniently close. She'd barely sent Dakota a text, telling her that she was right and sending her Deke's address, before he was opening the door to a shiny lobby, the kind that housed luxury apartments. All glass, no warmth.

Pretty fancy digs for a lumberjack.

"I'm subletting from a friend," he explained as he nodded to the concierge. An apartment building with a concierge. Definitely not the apartment of a lumberjack.

Deke's hand was at the small of her back, guiding her into the elevator. He leaned around her to press the button, but she didn't notice which floor because, uh, forearms.

"Jesus, you smell good." And he did. Sort of woodsy and manly.

He gave her a crooked smile and, yeah, she was being kind of dumb, saying things out loud that should have been inner monologue only, but what could she do? A few hours ago, lumberjacks weren't even in the running for guys who weren't her type who she should probably try to get it on with. Now, she knew otherwise.

Anyway, when had keeping her mouth shut ever solved anything? She'd kept her opinion to herself with Paul, and all the Pauls before him, and all that got her was single in a sports bar on a Saturday night. Ooo . . . and she was alliterative.

Before she could ponder more of her recent productive self-discovery, Deke had bent closer and brushed her hair aside and leaned into her neck and . . . and sniffed.

She wasn't sure if she was disappointed or completely fucking turned on.

"You smell good, too," he said, his face so close to hers she could almost feel his beard against her cheek.

She was definitely turned on. She was shaking with it.

"Good thing or that would have been weird, right?"

Aaaaaaand now she remembered why she kept her mouth shut.

Deke leaned back; not far, but far enough that she couldn't almost feel his stubble.

"Are you nervous?" he asked her, and his eyes looked concerned. Dark and turned on, but concerned.

"No, no," she started. But if she was going to speak, she might as well tell the truth. "Yeah. A little."

"We don't have to—"

"Oh no. Yes, we do. Otherwise Dakota will kill me."

A cute little furrow line appeared between his eyebrows. Hot and cute. She *had* to get this guy naked.

"No offense, but if you're only here because your friend made you . . ."

"No! No. That came out wrong. Dakota just . . . she just encouraged me. I want to be here. I want to do this." She ran her hands up his arms, bumping over ridges of muscle. "Oh God do I want to do this."

"Good." He started to lean into her, but then he stopped. Blergh. "Why did Dakota encourage you to do, uh, this?"

And then, before she could even formulate the thought that she should shut the hell up, it all came out in a breathless rush. "She says I really need to get laid. She says I go out with boring guys who don't know my ass from their elbow—her expression. And she's right. My boyfriends are boring. That's why it never works out, no matter how hard I try. Tonight, I just need to get my world rocked by a muscly stranger who can make me forget that boring Pauls even exist in the world. I just want my toes to curl. I want to feel the warm, hot weight of a naked man on top of me. I want to come until I stop breathing." She stopped, realizing that a lot more stuff had come out of her mouth than she'd intended. "So . . ." She fiddled with the button on the front of his flannel shirt, but she didn't look up at him. She couldn't. She'd just told him she wanted to orgasm to death.

"That's a lot of pressure."

"I know."

"We haven't even kissed yet. Not properly."

"Even if the night ends right now, this has been a hundred times more erotic than the past several years of my dating life."

"Still, I think we can do better than that."

"If you think you're up for it."

"I know I'm up for it." He nudged his hips into hers and, yup, he was up for it.

Then his hands were in her hair, surprisingly gentle but she got the message, and she tilted her head back and up to him and she was there waiting when his lips came down and met hers and . . .

The elevator dinged.

Foster cursed the gods of technology and time that made him break contact with Becky. But they were on his floor, and on his floor was his apartment, and in his apartment was his bed, and if she could talk him into this state of excitement in less than two minutes in the elevator, what was she going to do to him when they had all night? And no clothes?

He'd never typed the passcode on his door faster.

Well, not his door, a fact he was reminded of as he threw the door open in an attempt to really let the seduction begin, only to be thwarted by a stack of cardboard boxes.

He caught himself just in time. He didn't think he could act out all the stuff Becky had described if he broke his pelvis by tripping over his own unpacked crap. One bad experience with public undressing was enough for a guy.

"Sorry about the mess," he said as he tossed unboxed clothes back into boxes. "My stuff just arrived today."

"Wow." He watched her take in Brock's apartment. It was an impressive place, he had to admit:

the modern furniture, the big open room, the view. If he was going to stay, this would be the kind of place he would want. Low maintenance, and he could watch the sun set over the mountains.

"You're a terrible houseguest."

"Huh?"

"Is this what you call crashing at a friend's place?"

So she wasn't as dazzled by the modern amenities as he thought she was. She was right, though. If Brock was here, his friend would kill him. Hell, *he* wanted to kill him, and it was his stuff. He'd sold everything he didn't need when he'd left New York, and yet he was surrounded by boxes.

The mess stressed him out. He should have stayed in and unpacked. His palms were sweating just thinking about it.

Then Becky took off her jacket and tossed it on a pile of boxes and reached up and undid the clip in her hair. The blond waves fell over her shoulders, teasing the tops of her breasts.

Nope, he'd made the right decision going out tonight.

"What does your friend do when he wants to get to his couch?"

"First of all, there's a very clear trail to the couch." To prove it, he took her hand and led her through the valley of cardboard to the clean lines of the modern sofa. It wasn't the most comfortable couch, but it looked cool. He sat, pulled her down next to him, and wrapped his arm around her. Because the couch wasn't that comfortable and he wanted to be a good host.

Also, he liked the smell of her hair.

"Secondly," he said, propping his feet on the boxes that were closer than the coffee table. "Secondly, my friend isn't here; I'm subletting. Brock is on a year-long fellowship, traveling the world studying lace-making techniques."

"Wow. That's pretty cool."

"That's one of his things." He pointed to the framed lace hanging on the wall behind them. He wasn't sure if Brock had made it or repaired it or collected it or what. He kind of zoned out when Brock talked about lace. But Foster felt like he should make an effort because Brock was letting him sublet.

She twisted around. "Huh. If I asked you questions about it, would you be able to answer them?"

He was slightly distracted by the curve of her neck, but he managed a quick "nope."

"So you have a friend named Bullhorn and a friend named Brock."

"I do."

"How?"

He shrugged. "I don't know. Bullhorn was a frat brother—"

"Of course."

"—and I met Brock in grad school." He didn't like to throw around law school on a first date, if this even was a date. The women he went out with thought lawyers were a catch, and he wasn't here to be caught.

Well, caught for tonight.

"Grad school? What'd you study?"

He might not have a future with Becky, but he didn't want to lie to her.

So he didn't.

"What about that drink? I have delicious Denver tap water and possibly a beer." He tucked a strand of hair behind her ear. She shivered.

"You promised me orange juice."

"Right. I believe I said maybe orange juice."

"Semantics."

"Why are we talking about orange juice?" He leaned in.

"I'm not sure." She met him in the middle, her breath brushing across his lips.

"I thought you came up here to ravage me?" She was fiddling with something, but he couldn't stop looking at her lips long enough to see.

"I'm pretty sure you're supposed to do the ravaging," she said and shuffled just out of his reach.

"We can ravage each other."

He was going to take a moment to congratulate himself on his quick wordplay—he wasn't, generally speaking, a funny guy—but he found himself with a Becky on his lap, and this Becky had no shirt on.

Good lord. That bra. "That bra is magical."

"Wait 'til you see what's underneath it," she said, and that was it. The ravaging was on. He pulled her close and put his mouth on every square inch of her he could reach. She was soft and sweet, and she gasped and arched under his touch.

"I don't think we should have sex on Brock's

couch," she gasped into his mouth. She was right. So he stood, and she squealed but held on tight as he walked them back to the bedroom.

Then he dropped her on the bed and she bounced and, holy shit, she was gorgeous. He climbed over her, but she pushed him off and reached for the button of his jeans.

"Yes," he said. She was smart. He reached for the button of hers.

It took a minute because they kept getting in each other's way, but soon their pants were off and he'd thrown his shirt over his head. She took the moment he was off balance to roll over him. She straddled his hips and ran her fingers up and down his chest.

"Wow," she said as she traced each line of muscle. "Is this real?" She leaned down and bit his pec.

"Ow!"

"Sorry." She kissed it better, then kissed a trail of kisses across his chest, down his stomach, down . . .

Oh God. He was pretty sure he was in love.

But before he fell too much in love, she had climbed back up. "Condom?" she asked as her hair made a curtain around their faces. He rolled over far enough to reach the nightstand, then remembered he wasn't in his apartment, which had condoms in the nightstand. He thought quickly, which was difficult with Becky wiggling on top of him.

"Never mind." She jumped off him and off the bed and dug in the pocket of her jeans. "Ta-da!"

She climbed back on him, wielding her treasure. "Ready?" she asked, and all he could do was grunt because her hands were on him, and then she was on him, and then he was inside her, and they both gasped and rocked and cried out and, holy God, he was definitely in love.

Chapter Three

Becky woke up warm.

Her ideal conditions for falling asleep were a freezing room and a big blanket to cuddle under. This usually resulted in her waking up with cold toes, after having kicked her blankets off in the middle of the night. She was a restless sleeper. Maybe because her room was usually so cold that her body took advantage of her being unconscious to do some calisthenics for warmth. At least that was what Dakota thought. But Dakota only thought that because Dakota liked to fall asleep in a sauna.

So it was strange that she was so warm. She also thought her room smelled weird. Not bad, but not like fresh linens and lightly scented candles. This morning, her room smelled . . . musky. Kind of like a man.

All at once it registered: Her room smelled weird because it wasn't her room, and she was warm because she was draped in naked man. Naked lumberjack with whom she'd had a toe-curling one-night stand.

Yay, lumberjack.

She owed Dakota, like, forty-five soy lattes. She was so right. Becky felt totally reset.

She should have one-night stands more often.

With the lumberjack.

No, no, not with the lumberjack. There were other lumberjacks in the sea, surely. One-night stand meant no more nights.

It also probably meant no mornings either. She didn't have a ton of experience with them—a little, but not a ton—and it wasn't called a one-night-and-a-morning stand. A twelve-hour stand. A call-your-doctor-if-your-one-night-stand-lasts-more-than-twenty-four-hours stand.

She should leave.

Waa, leaving.

There was a big part of her that wanted to stay. He was a really good cuddler, the way his thigh was pressed up against her, his chest curled around her back, one arm across her waist, cupping her breast like it was the most natural thing in the world. It was comfortable. Plus, it brought back fond memories of the night before, when he was not so gentle, and her toes curled again at the memory.

But she should go. If she stayed, she would fall in love, and she had promised Dakota that she wouldn't. This was just supposed to be a positive-sex moment, and boy howdy was it ever. She didn't want to ruin it by getting to know the guy, because, as Dakota rightly pointed out, getting to know the guy had always ruined her positive-sex moments because she had terrible taste in men. If she got to know him and liked him, he wasn't worth getting to know.

But if she stayed, just a little bit longer, they could have toe-curling morning sex. And she'd be able to see all that lumberjack gorgeousness in the daylight. She'd bet he'd feel even better if she could see him.

No. She had to be strong. She had to go.

She could just sneak one more look at him, though. She could do that without waking him up.

Of course, he had her breast in his hand. She kind of needed that back.

Moving like the stealth jungle cat she was—thank goodness he was a heavy sleeper, though the poor guy had earned it, she thought, her toes curling yet again—she rolled slowly onto her stomach. His hand, floppy with sleep, traced her movements: her chest, her shoulder, her back. She tried her best not to shiver with pleasure by focusing on being a stealth jungle cat, and she kept rolling until she was on her other side, facing him.

God he was cute.

Whatever tension she'd seen in his face in the bar the night before was gone, the line between his eyebrows smoothed out in sleep. She remembered how that line had deepened as he concentrated on her, and rather than let her reflexive toe curling convince her that maybe she really could go after they had a morning positive-sex moment, she shifted her butt so it was hanging off the bed, then bent a leg down until her foot hit the floor, then slid out and into a squat. He shifted in his sleep, snuffled into her vacated pillow, and she dropped down to the floor. Because he definitely wouldn't be able to see her, what with her being a stealth jungle cat and also a morning-after ninja.

She ignored the way his hair stood up at wonky angles in the back in a very cute, sleepy way, and the way the muscles in his shoulders bunched and relaxed in a very sexy way. She almost willed him to wake up, he looked so perfect.

That, ultimately, was what propelled her to grab her underwear—how did it end up on top of the dresser?—dig her shirt out from behind the couch—how???—and sneak out the door as soon as she was decent enough to do so.

As the door closed behind her, she took a deep breath. As she exhaled, she expelled any feelings of regret she felt at leaving that perfect, perfectly naked lumberjackian male specimen alone in his warm, warm bed. She was left a little light-headed and a lot in need of coffee, but as she took the elevator down to the street and found her car, she had a decided bounce to her step. Positive-sex moment: accomplished.

She was reset and ready to find her settle-down guy.

Who wasn't a lumberjack.

Well, not *that* lumberjack. But this was good information. This had opened up a whole new kind of guy to discover. She called Dakota to let her know she was still alive, and that they needed to figure out how to infiltrate the timber industry.

* * *

Foster woke up and stretched like he'd never needed to stretch in his life. How was he so tired, even though he'd just slept like a log? That might have been the best sleep of his life. Definitely the best sleep he'd had since moving back to Denver.

Then it started coming back to him. The bar, the blonde, the minds blown.

Becky. Becky in all her sweet, toe-curling, back-clutching, name-shouting glory.

Where was she? He ran his hands over the side of the bed, where he was pretty sure he'd left her, but, nope, his eyes did not deceive him. She was gone, and the pillow was cold. But it still smelled like her. He inhaled.

So he was now both a detective and a psycho.

Maybe she was in the shower. Brock's place had an amazing shower. Three showerheads, heated floor, tile bench. It was like a carwash in there. Plenty of room for two.

But when he got to the bathroom, the shower was empty.

Disappointed, he threw on last night's jeans—how did they get halfway under the mattress?—and headed toward the kitchen. Maybe she was making coffee. Naked. Or an omelet. He could go for an omelet. And coffee. And Becky wearing nothing but an apron . . .

But, no, she wasn't in the kitchen either. She wasn't on the not-very-comfortable couch watching

TV. He went back to the bedroom, but, no, she wasn't there.

He knew he was getting desperate when he checked for her in the hall closet. But he checked anyway.

She wasn't there.

She was gone.

He flopped down on a not-very-comfortable chair that matched the sofa. Hmph.

Well, this was probably for the best. He didn't want anything serious, and if she'd stayed, it could have gotten serious. Hell, if she had been naked and making coffee, it definitely would have gotten serious.

He rubbed his hands over his face. Definitely good she'd left.

Well, naked coffee obviously wasn't going to make itself, so he got up and headed to the kitchen. Then he thought she might have left her number. He looked around for a scrap of paper in the sea of boxes. If it was there, he'd never find it. Even more reason for him to finish unpacking.

But first, coffee. He'd gotten a serious workout last night—man, he hoped she'd left her number— and he seriously needed to caffeinate.

As the coffee brewed, he leaned against the counter island and watched out the windows as the clouds drift over the mountains. You didn't get views like this in New York, he reminded himself. Maybe it wasn't terrible to be back.

His phone rang and he grabbed it.

"Oh good, you're up."

"Hi, Mom."

"Don't sound so disappointed, love."

He wasn't disappointed. He hadn't thought, in a momentary flash of joy, that Becky had somehow retrieved his number from his phone and was now calling him to schedule some more time of not getting serious.

But now he was on the phone with his mother.

So he needed to reset.

"Sorry; it's early." He looked at the clock on the microwave. Not that early, but, well, he didn't need to get into that.

"I suppose you're technically on vacation."

He snorted.

"Don't snort, dear."

He rolled his eyes.

"And don't roll your eyes."

"How did you . . . never mind. What's up?"

"It's your sister."

He tensed. There could be no good news about Madison this early in the morning.

"She's at the pound."

The pound? Was that another name for jail? Was his mother suddenly using slang?

Then he remembered the pound wasn't really *the pound*, but rather an animal shelter run by the county and some local nonprofits, and the current location where Madison was working off her community service hours.

She must be serious about getting reformed if she was going to the animal shelter this early in the morning.

Well, not that early.

Focus, Foster.

"OK. So, uh . . . what does that have to do with me?" He tried not to sound petulant, but he hadn't had caffeine and his mother was being obscure.

"I have a meeting this afternoon, so I'll need you to pick her up."

"What if I have plans?" Which he would, if he could successfully track down Becky.

"I suppose she could have someone at the shelter drive her home. I just hate to think what would happen if she was unattended all afternoon. . . ."

Foster knew the beginning of a guilt trip when he heard it.

And his mother wasn't wrong. Madison was turning out to be a trouble magnet. His mother seemed to think, though, that it was all because of the bad influence of her miscreant friends. Because there was no way the girl who got kicked out of church choir when she was ten for a spontaneous solo that rhymed Christmas with some unfortunate biological functions was, as a teenager, able to come up with ways to break the rules on her own. Except now she wasn't just doing crazy things because she was chafing at authority or wanted attention. Now she was doing actual stupid, illegal things, like drinking way too young.

And that was just the stuff she got caught at.

Foster hadn't been a great older brother. He was embarrassed when his mother was pregnant with Madison, and he couldn't relate to the little kid who followed him everywhere and was too annoying to be any fun. She was barely in school when he left for college. But somehow, that separation made them closer. When he hardly saw her, when she wasn't constantly under his feet, that was when he was able to step back and think that she was kind of an OK person.

And, fine, the hero worship was good for his ego.

No matter what, though, Madison was his sister. He knew what it was like growing up with Lydia and Andrew Deacon and their high expectations. A Deacon doesn't let someone else win captain of the lacrosse team. A Deacon doesn't let someone else win valedictorian. A Deacon doesn't let someone else win, period.

Madison was his kid sister, and whether he liked it or not—or whether he deserved it or not—she looked up to him. He had a responsibility to exert whatever good influence he had over her to make sure she didn't totally screw up.

If nothing else, he could show her how to drink and not get caught.

He poured himself a cup of coffee, cradling the phone between his ear and his shoulder. He took a sip, braced himself. "No, Mom, you're right. I'll pick her up. We'll grab some lunch."

"Better make it dinner."

He wasn't going to find Becky anyway. Time to let it go and man up. He was only going to be here for a little while, after all.

"OK. Dinner."

He brought his coffee over to the not-very-comfortable couch and listened to his mother tell him all about the charity meeting she was about to attend—complete with a mention of all the eligible daughters and granddaughters of the members— and looked at his boxes, willing them unpacked. Maybe he'd shave his vacation beard today. He kind of liked it. He liked that Becky liked it. Which, aside from its being unprofessional, was a great reason to get rid of it.

At least he had a great view.

Chapter Four

Becky flipped through her camera bag before she got out of the car. Flash, check. Wide lens, check. Squeaky toy, check.

She put the bag of homemade peanut butter dog treats in her pocket. She had made the mistake of putting them in her camera bag exactly once. Fortunately, the only damage was to the bag itself, but still . . . Camera bags weren't cheap, and she couldn't bear to put a dog in a situation where he felt like misbehavior was the only option. Removing barriers to homemade peanut butter dog treats, for example. It wasn't the dog's fault there was an expensive camera bag in the way.

Just before she shut the door, she grabbed her sunglasses. She was still a bit foggy from her late night and early morning—she shivered a little just thinking about it. When she got home after sneaking out of Deke's apartment like a cat-burgling maniac, she'd very much wanted to get under her covers and stay there. At least until she had to get up for work on Monday.

But she'd been coming to the New Hope Animal Sanctuary every Sunday afternoon for a little over a year now, ever since Dakota got the job as director. Part of her hated it; it broke her heart every time she left those little doggie faces behind, but she wasn't allowed to have pets in her apartment. Still, the painful thought of quitting totally outweighed any sadness she felt. For one thing, the hurt Dakota would inflict on her for not showing up would probably be very real. But more importantly, she couldn't imagine not doing whatever she could to help these pathetic little love bugs find homes.

She couldn't adopt them, but she could photograph them.

And she had, every other weekend for a year now. She took well-lit, well-posed photos, and the shelter posted them on social media, and *boom*, the adoption rate had increased by 20 percent—which was a lot!—but it wasn't enough. People continued to be dumb with animals, abandoning them or worse. New Hope continued stepping in to help.

"Heads-up!"

Becky ducked just as a Frisbee whizzed by her ear. *That was a close call*, she thought as she straightened up. But being a little off-balance only put her even more directly in the line of the charging pit bull.

"Ack!" she said, raising her camera up to protect the expensive gear as she went down, her back getting wet with mud, her front getting covered in slobbery kisses.

"Rizzo, off!" she heard Maddie call. Rizzo planted her paws on Becky's chest and got down to business, searching for the source of the peanut butter smell.

"Are you kidding me? Rizzo!" She heard Maddie run toward them. Becky flipped off the lens cap and snapped a few quick shots. The angle wouldn't be great, but adorableness in action was an effective marketing tool.

"Rizzo, off," Maddie said to Rizzo's face. Becky looked up and took a shot of Maddie. She'd probably hate it—didn't all teenage girls hate pictures of themselves?—but Becky thought it would do her good to see how authoritative she looked when the dogs listened to her.

Rizzo whimpered and climbed off. Then the dog noticed the Frisbee lying in the grass and went nuts trying to pick it up.

"Sorry," Maddie said, giving Becky a hand up. "Bad throw."

"Well, you missed, kid."

"In my defense, you did say 'yes' when I asked if you were ready to catch it."

Becky didn't recall hearing that Maddie was about to throw a plastic disc at her head. If she had, she definitely would have said no because her hands were full of camera.

In Maddie's defense, Becky had been a little distracted. By Deke. The lumberjack of her dreams.

She shivered.

"You OK?" Maddie asked.

Yup, just having aftershocks from a night of getting thoroughly, royally, and athletically boinked.

That was probably not an appropriate thing to say to a teenage volunteer. She knew Maddie was no innocent—and was she a volunteer when it was court-ordered?—but still. Becky felt like she should at least pretend to be a good role model.

"Just distracted," Becky told her. That was true. Maddie didn't need to know why.

"Are you getting sick or something? Your face looks kind of red."

Becky knew her cheeks were flushing, on account of remembering all that thorough and athletic stuff—

"No, I mean—" Maddie made a circle around her mouth. "Like beard burn."

Becky felt her cheeks get even hotter. She didn't need to be talking to a sixteen-year-old about beard burn.

"I always put Vaseline on it."

"Doesn't that make you break out?" Becky said, mentally scanning her medicine cabinet. "Also, why are you making out with people old enough to give you beard burn?"

Maddie shrugged. "Some guys in my class developed early."

"Maddie—"

Maddie held up her hands. "No, please. Don't give me the safe-sex talk. I've heard it from my mom, two aunts, and last weekend my brother came home and, man, that was awkward."

"You have a brother?"

"Yeah. He lived in New York, but he had to move back here for work."

"Oh?"

Maddie rolled her eyes with impressive teenage disdain. "And, he says, to keep me out of trouble."

Becky snorted. "Good luck." But inside, she melted a little. That was sweet; a big brother coming home to take care of his kid sister. Plus, he saw the smile Maddie tried to hide. He must be a good big brother.

Unless he was a controlling alphahole, in which case he deserved all the hell Maddie's sixteen-year-old attitude threw at him.

"Hey, I'm not the one so gaga over some bearded dude that I'm getting hit with Frisbees."

"I'm not gaga." Becky was decidedly not gaga. That was the whole point. One night only. She'd gotten her gaga out last night.

"So who was he? A hot date? Are you going to see him again?"

Because the answers were *I don't really know; not a date, a one-night stand;* and *no*, Becky changed the subject. "Is Rizzo our first victim?"

"What, you don't want to be a good female role model and show me what a healthy and appropriate relationship looks like?"

"What, you want Rizzo to spend another week in the shelter?"

"Gah! You're getting way too good at guilt trips."

Becky smiled triumphantly.

"You sound like my mother," Maddie said.

Becky deflated, just a little, at Maddie's tone. She'd never met Maddie's mother, but she knew that wasn't a compliment. Becky didn't know much about Maddie's home life, but she'd been working with her long enough to know it wasn't good. She got dropped off and picked up by a big, shiny SUV and she had a phone that was way nicer than anything Becky would even dream of spending money on, but when a kid as young as Maddie was doing community service . . . well, something was up.

Becky knew what it was like growing up in a house where nobody understood you. She had coped by keeping her head down and barely meeting everybody's low expectations of her. She would never in a million years have acted out the way Maddie did; that would have drawn too much attention to her, and the last thing Becky wanted was attention.

Still, she recognized teenage-girl drama when she saw it. Sisterhood of the hormonal and all that.

But she wasn't here to be Maddie's mentor. She wasn't even her supervisor; Dakota had assured her of that when Maddie started. But, well, the more time she spent with her and her alleged bad attitude, the more she liked her. Especially because the kid hadn't met a dog she didn't love into blissful submission.

Maddie whistled and Rizzo came trotting over with the now-destroyed Frisbee.

"I'm going to check in," Becky told her, giving Rizzo a quick scratch as she walked by. "You get Rizzo set up in the enclosure on the hill." Although the whole place was fenced in, it was much easier to capture a good shot when the dogs had a slightly limited place to run. Besides, the spot on the hill had an old stone wall and some great tree trunks. Rizzo would get to show off her explorer side, making her appealing to potential hikers. And in Denver, there were quite a few.

Maddie nodded and jogged through the yard, Rizzo following happily behind her. The kid really did have a way with dogs.

She walked toward the shelter office, brushing the dirt off her jeans. She didn't know why she bothered; she was going to get covered in mud and dog slobber again as soon as she started the shoot. But, well, she had a professional aesthetic to uphold.

She caught a glimpse of herself in the reflective glass of the door. Flyaway hair, chapped lips, and her flannel was buttoned wrong. Very professional.

Fixing her shirt, she went inside, expecting to see one of the other volunteers at the reception desk.

"Hello?" she called into the void.

"Be right there!"

Becky followed the voice to the puppy room, where Dakota was doing her second job, after acting as Becky's pimp, as the executive director of New Hope. She and two of the burlier kennel workers were trying to maneuver a small dog carrier into a larger cage.

Dakota turned and nodded at Becky. "Give us a second. We've got a freak-out over here. Put it down, guys; she's not coming out."

There was a loud yip as the crate rested on the

ground. "Maybe undo the top? Let her calm down a little before you take it off."

The burlier of the burlies got down on the floor and started quietly unscrewing the bolts that were holding the top of the plastic crate to the bottom. While he worked, he spoke nonsense words in a surprisingly gentle voice.

"She was just dropped off," Dakota explained quietly.

"Not abused?" Becky asked hopefully. She hated the abuse cases. She hated that they'd be at the shelter longer because they were so afraid of people. It made her get all ragey.

Dakota shook her head. Becky stood down.

"Her owner went into a nursing home."

"Poor girl," Becky said. No wonder she was freaking out.

"The Realtor found her hiding under a bed when she went to list the house. She'd been there all alone for three days."

Becky's hand went right up to her mouth to stifle whatever loud, sad noise she was about to make.

At first Becky didn't think there was a dog inside when Mr. Burly lifted the top off the crate. Just some ratty old blanket. Then the blanket moved, and two tiny black eyes locked with hers. Becky saw sadness and fear and confusion in those watery little eyes, and she found herself blinking back tears.

Maybe she could keep this one. Maybe her landlord wouldn't notice.

"Come on, little Starr," Dakota said, putting her gloves back on and slowly approaching the open crate. Starr huddled in the corner, shivering, her matted fur shaking. Dakota bent down and reached for her. Becky held her breath.

Starr didn't bite—that was a good sign—but she didn't move either. Still, Dakota was able to scoop her up to put her into the open cage.

"Sweet girl," Dakota murmured, and Becky watched how Starr melted right into her, her little doggy head resting on Dakota's shoulder. "Jesus, I hate to put you in here, my love." But without knowing anything about her, they couldn't just let her run free. Becky knew that; she'd asked about it before.

But now she was getting choked up. Before she rendered herself entirely unable to take pictures, she scooted out of the room and waited for Dakota in the lobby.

She came out a few minutes later. "Well, that sucked. I'm glad to see you, though."

"I can't believe that poor little dog was in such bad shape."

"I know. But little fluffy white dogs have no problem getting adopted, so hopefully we can clean her up and get her out of here soon. And no, you can't take her home. I know your building's rules."

"I wasn't going to—"

Dakota just shook her head and gave her a rueful smile. "You do enough. You don't need to make yourself homeless, too. Anyway, you think you can do eight or ten today?"

"It'll be tight."

"It'll require the stamina of a lumberjack."

If Becky's camera wasn't so expensive, she would

have thrown it at Dakota's head. She cursed her morning oversharing, then cursed the lovemaking lumberjack who'd caused her to get a late start in the first place. Then she uncursed him, because, well, it just didn't seem right.

"We can do it," she assured Dakota once she was done shooting daggers at her. "Maddie's out there with Rizzo, so can someone bring the next model in about twenty minutes?" That wasn't much time, but Rizzo knew her a little, so it shouldn't take as long as it usually did to get the dog comfortable with her camera.

Becky couldn't stop thinking about Starr as she walked out to the enclosure, where Maddie and Rizzo were waiting. It would be a while before the little fluffball was ready to be adopted and Becky hoped she got the chance to photograph her next weekend.

Then Rizzo saw her, and in addition to being a Frisbee enthusiast, she also turned out to be a born model, posing and hamming it up so perfectly, Maddie had almost no corralling to do. It allowed Becky to put Starr to the back of her mind for now.

With the sad little mop dog and the sexy lumberjack, the back of her mind was getting awfully crowded.

"Hey, squirt. Rob any banks today?"

Madison rolled her eyes at Foster as she climbed

into his SUV. It was an old joke between them. He realized now that it was probably time to retire it.

Not that Madison had robbed a bank. But she had been arrested for underage drinking when her friend got pulled over for driving recklessly. Just thinking about it made his palms sweat.

But Madison didn't need to be reminded of how stupid the whole thing had been. And she'd seemed more subdued since then, as if she was, for once, thinking about the consequences of her actions.

Or maybe it was because every time she sneezed, their mother gave her a lecture.

Still, she seemed to like her community service. Did that defeat the purpose? he wondered. It was supposed to be a punishment. Maybe Maddie, for once, had gotten lucky. She got to learn a lesson *and* find some fulfillment that didn't involve breaking a law. He wasn't sure what it involved, but it wasn't illegal.

"What do you do in there all day?" he asked her. "Just walk dogs?"

"No. I also pick up their shit."

"Hey. Language."

Madison stuck out her tongue.

They rode in silence for a moment. Foster wanted to say something meaningful, something that would get his sister's head out of her ass and get her to quit being such a brat. Because if she didn't, she'd be a felonious brat, and there was only so much a family of lawyers could do to help her then.

That wasn't true. Their dad could probably get

her out of any legal trouble she found herself in, wielding the powerful connections he'd cultivated from all those years of being a shitty father.

Yeah, he was a shitty father, and Foster got why Madison was acting out. But he'd never done the kind of crap she pulled. No, that wasn't true. He'd gotten into plenty of trouble. He'd just never gotten caught. And, really, was it right to call it trouble if there were no consequences? Wasn't the nature of trouble defined by not just the breaking of the rules but being caught in the act?

By that logic, if he had killed someone—a big if—would it be murder if he wasn't caught? Sure, it would. But it wouldn't be trouble. So he'd be a murderer, but he wouldn't be in trouble.

"Quit arguing with yourself."

"Hmm?" Had he said that aloud? Yikes, he didn't need to give Madison any tips on causing mayhem without getting caught.

"You've got that lawyer face on. Like when you and Dad go at it at dinner."

"I don't have a lawyer face."

"Yeah, you do. You and Dad both have it. It comes out when you guys start arguing over whether that bank guy in Aurora was really responsible for all those people losing their houses."

"He willfully misled the homeowners—"

"Yeah, yeah, I know. I was there. Then Dad was like, *it was all laid out in the contracts they signed*, and you were like, *but they were written in language designed to mislead* and blah blah blah, who cares, people lost their houses!"

"I didn't know you were paying attention."

"I tried not to, but what was I gonna do, talk to Mom?"

"You could try it."

"No, thanks. Besides, you guys were arguing over little tiny words, which I'm pretty sure the people who are now homeless don't give a shit about."

"Language."

"I'm serious. Who cares about a word or two when people are losing their houses?"

"They lost their houses because of a clever lawyer who cared about that word or two."

"Yeah, but the point is, you and Dad weren't arguing whether the banker was wrong, but whether the words made a difference."

"So?"

"So! You think those people in court cared about semantics?"

"I think they did, because semantics won them the case. Also, semantics? That's a pretty big word for you."

"I'm not an idiot. And I'm not arguing with you just so you can win."

"That's not why I'm arguing. I'm just pointing out—"

"Please, please, don't lecture me! I'm saying this totally shady guy was doing something shitty and you're arguing about words instead of the fact that, hey, maybe people shouldn't be so shitty to each other. And yes, I know, *language*."

Foster shouldn't have egged her on like that. Madison was still a kid. Of course she wasn't going to be able to set the ethical implications aside to enjoy the legal puzzle in the case. He remembered when he was that naïve. He would get so frustrated with his father, who'd spin an argument around his teenage head until Foster didn't know which way was up, and then he'd always get in a parting shot, just to make sure Foster knew who was smarter.

He resisted the urge to get in the last word with Madison.

Although it was hard.

"Can you drop me off at Dylan's?"

"No. Who's Dylan?"

"What do you mean, no! You're just picking me up because Mom didn't want to drive all the way out here."

"That's not true. Who's Dylan?"

"She's a girl from school."

"A girl named Dylan?"

"Yes. God, don't be such an old fart."

"I am not—" He stopped himself. Even he, who never met an argument he didn't like, could see that there was no sense in trying to convince a sixteen-year-old that he wasn't old. "I'm taking you out to dinner—that's why I'm not taking you to Dylan's."

"Can we bring Dylan?"

"You're not too embarrassed to have your friends see you with your old-fart brother?"

"Shut up."

"Too bad, because we're here." He pulled into the lot of a new gourmet pizza place. He'd Yelped it and it had good reviews. None of them explicitly said it was a good place to have a forced heart-to-heart with your troubled teenage sister, but never mind that.

They got their table and placed their order. Madison fiddled with her silverware. He looked around the restaurant, as if it might contain clues about how to deal with teenage emotions.

"You should get a dog."

Well, that was one way to start.

"Why should I get a dog?" He'd like to get one, but it had seemed cruel to have one in New York. Denver was a great place for a dog, though. Too bad he wasn't sticking around.

Madison shrugged. "Dogs are great. And there are so many great dogs at the shelter. You could save a dog's life."

"If I got a dog, it wouldn't be some random shelter dog."

"Don't be gross. Shelter dogs are great. It's just people who are dumb."

"Shelter people?"

"No, people who abandon their dogs. But seriously, there are so many great dogs there."

"So you've said."

"Today, Becky and I—"

"Becky?"

"Yeah, she's the photographer."

His heart started to beat a little faster. But surely there was more than one Becky in Denver.

"Don't look so weird; she's a positive influence. She's old, like you."

He threw his crumpled up straw wrapper at her.

"What does she look like?"

"Gross."

"No, I mean I know someone named Becky. I wonder if it's the same one."

"What's her last name?"

"Ah . . . I'm not sure."

"Ew, no. I do not want to hear about this random Becky. My Becky is old and she wears combat boots."

"Is she blonde?"

"You're seriously pissing me off. No, she's not blonde."

"Ah." He tried not to feel disappointed. Because, really, what were the chances?

"If you're done being a creepy horndog . . . ?"

"I wasn't—never mind. What about you and Becky?"

"She takes photos of the shelter dogs so they can get adopted more quickly and I help her out. And today we had a marathon. There's this one dog who would be perfect for you . . ."

As Madison waxed on about the perfection of each of the dogs she worked with, Foster got a worried feeling in the pit of his stomach. She was attached to pretty much all of them. And he was going to adopt absolutely none of them.

Not because they were shelter dogs. Because he didn't want to get a dog.

Not now anyway.

"Why don't you adopt one?" he asked. Having a dog would teach her responsibility, probably. He'd bet he could convince his mother of that.

"Please, you think Mom's gonna let me bring home some mutt?"

"I thought they were perfect."

"They are perfect, but Mom's a snob. You're not."

"I'm subletting. I don't think Brock would appreciate me bringing a dog into his home without checking with him first."

"So check. Brock loves dogs. And I'll help clean up any messes the dog makes, I promise."

That seemed likely.

But if he got a dog, he could hold Madison to that promise. And it would be a reason for them to spend more time together without her trying to ditch him for Dylan or whoever. So he could be a positive influence and teach her responsibility.

Of course he'd have to live with the dog. And what would he do with it when he left?

Still, he couldn't outright say no to his kid sister.

"Let me think about it."

She squealed and clapped her hands, and it was the first time he'd seen her genuinely happy since . . . well, since he didn't know when.

He smiled back. Their pizza arrived. He could have the serious emotional conversation later. For now, he'd just have dinner with his happy little sister.

Chapter Five

"Ugh, Mondays, amirite?"

Becky looked up from her computer to see one of the mail guys, Will, leaning against the doorframe of her sad, windowless office.

"Good morning, Will." It was eleven, so, technically it *was* still morning. And for Will, eleven was early. He was usually stumbling into work around this time, and they'd be lucky to get their mail by the time he rolled out at five. But Will was Mr. Glassmeyer's grandson, and nepotism was alive and well in the field of corporate law, which meant Will could come in whenever he wanted. In most places, this would make Will the most hated man in the office, or at least in the mailroom. But Becky had learned through the office grapevine that Mr. Glassmeyer made sure his coworkers' paychecks were inversely proportionate to the amount of work Will did.

This also made her feel a lot less guilty for liking the guy, pain in the ass that he was.

"Don't remind me." Will put a stack of interoffice

envelopes on her desk. She moved them to her inbox. The inbox that was clearly marked on the corner of her desk. But, well. He was Will. What could she do?

It was like clockwork, in the sense that a broken clock is still right twice a day. And twice a day, when she was eyeballs deep in Westlaw, Will would come in and deliver the mail. He'd put it all on her desk, she'd throw him a don't-interrupt-me look, he'd come in and sit down to ramble and gossip, then he'd go away and she'd distribute the mail to the other librarians. She realized this part was Will's job, but she'd quickly learned it was easier to just do it herself. Besides, Will had good gossip.

Today, Becky couldn't afford the distraction. She had a partner breathing down her neck for precedents involving the National Register of Historic Places, which was just the kind of research she didn't like to ask too many questions about—besides, even if she did ask, they never told her—but the fact that it was urgent made Becky a little uneasy.

On second thought, maybe a gossip break would help ease the headache that was building behind her right eye.

Anyway, Becky had learned that Will didn't require much interaction. If she just gave an occasional non-committal grunt, he would entertain himself and she could keep working.

"New guy starts today," Will said. He'd plucked the pen with the big pink pom-pom from the cup on her desk and was rubbing it slowly across his forehead. That was a distraction too far.

She reached over to grab the pen from him.

"Hey! I was using that!"

"Will, how many times do I have to tell you not to come in here and molest my office supplies?"

"That's the magic pom-pom pen. It cures my hangovers."

She rolled her eyes at him. Suggesting that he not drink so much on a work night was nothing but a waste of breath. She knew that from experience. "Get your own pom-pom pen."

"You're just mad because you forgot the new guy started today."

"Why would I be mad about that? And how do you know the new guy is a guy?"

Will raised an eyebrow. "Um, because his picture came with the press release."

Oh, right. She remembered now. She hadn't paid much attention because she was still living under the happy delusion that Paul was the love of her life.

Huh. The little pang of sadness she usually felt when she thought about Paul was gone. In fact, this was the first time she'd thought about Paul since Saturday. Which meant her magical lumberjack sexual reset had totally worked.

"Besides, if you had remembered he was coming, you would have worn a cuter outfit."

"What's wrong with my outfit?"

"Nothing, but whenever there's a new guy, you get all dolled up."

"Will, you're being disgusting." She pretended the heat suffusing her face was all righteous indignation and not embarrassment that Will had figured out her stupid attempts to impress new guys at work. They all did it, all the women who worked in the library. Even the married ones. It was the patriarchy, she decided. It was the patriarchy that made them get dolled up because it had been instilled in them that it was their biological duty to seek the approval of men.

That was it. The patriarchy.

Not that it matters now, she thought. She'd sworn off boring lawyers, and no amount of patriarchy could talk her out of that, so it didn't matter that she was wearing the slacks that were maybe a little snugger in the waist than she preferred and a blouse that didn't quite hide the fact that her slacks were too snug in the waist. And that she'd had a wash-and-go morning with her hair instead of taking the time to blow it dry and relatively flat. And that she hadn't bothered with makeup beyond a swipe of mascara.

Nope. Didn't matter one bit. When she met this new guy, whoever he was, she would present the image that she was a professional colleague without the potential for anything more, because that was what she was. A colleague. She didn't sleep with lawyers anymore.

No, now her fantasies were reserved for lumberjacks. Not for Deke the Lumberjack specifically, because that ship had sailed. She was a one-trip-on-a-ship gal now. Oh, maybe pirates were a thing she could get into. Lumberjacks, pirates . . . the world was her sexual oyster. As long as he didn't wear a boring suit, and definitely not if he was a lawyer.

"You're literally the only woman in the office not totally dazzled by the great Foster Deacon."

Foster Deacon? A little bell went off in the back of her head, like she'd heard that name before. And she had: His name was always listed on those Thirty-Under-30 things that talked about what a genius he was, and it was pretty much all Mr. Polak could talk about since the guy had signed a contract with P&G. But that wasn't it. It was something else.

Maybe it was because the name Deacon made her think of Deke, but that was some next-level wishful thinking there. There was no way a legal whiz would have a beard like that. Besides, there were lots of Deacons in the world. Probably.

"You OK, Beck? You look like you're in pain."

"Ha! What? No! I'm just . . . I'm very busy."

She pulled up the P&G web site and searched through the press releases—just in case—for the one announcing the arrival of Foster Deacon, legal whiz. She'd just clicked on it when she heard voices come into the library. She recognized Mr. Polak, the senior partner who would be seriously unimpressed with Will's chill work ethic. Why was her stupid internet so slow? Anne never should have gotten into that political argument with the guy from IT. The text loaded, but she kind of knew that part. She knew this guy was some hotshot intellectual property guy, hired away from a big New York firm to build up their IP division. His hiring directly coincided with a whole mess of new research they'd barely scratched the surface of. She knew his arrival had something to do with the megacompany

Goliath, but obviously the press release didn't go into that. If they weren't going to tell the press, they weren't going to tell the librarians. Wait, that wasn't necessarily true; it just felt that way a lot of the time. Holy crap, why was her internet so slow!

She'd gotten just enough of a glance at his picture to notice that Foster Deacon was a vaguely familiar white guy—so, basically, any lawyer in the state of Colorado—when Mr. Polak was at the door with the white guy himself.

Her first thought was that this guy must be big news if Mr. Polak was showing him around. Usually, if new hires were shown around at all, Linda from HR did it. And Linda didn't take the person to everyone's office; she'd just stick her head in the library and say, "Here it is," and it would take weeks for the new associates to learn her name, or even to learn that she was not, in fact, just a really old intern.

"Hiya, Mr. P." Will had somehow regained possession of her pom-pom pen and was now tilting the chair back on two legs, out of her reach. She should just give him the damn pen. She didn't have to look at Mr. Polak to know he was fuming with annoyance. It was how Mr. Polak always looked at Will.

Not a great first impression that Will was goofing off in her office with her goofy pen, making her look like a goof by association.

But there was no time to think about her reputation. Because she was looking at the real-life Foster Deacon and he was making her wish she hadn't just put a firm ban on ever dating a lawyer again. Foster

Deacon was, in a word, *delicious.* And . . . he did look vaguely familiar. But how could he? She just had Deke on the brain, that was all. Foster Deacon didn't have a beard; Deke did. Deke also had piercing eyes that bored right into her soul as he hovered over her; Foster Deacon's eyes were just . . . piercing. Oh God.

No. It couldn't be. Just because Foster Deacon and Deke both had high cheekbones and dark eyebrows and sexy ears. Lots of people had sexy ears.

"And here is one of the librarians you'll be working with." Foster Deacon's gaze shifted to her just as Will's chair came crashing down, nearly dumping him at Mr. Polak's feet. So it took her a second to realize he was holding his hand out for her to shake, and then it took her another second to realize she definitely recognized that hand. That hand had done amazing things to her. She couldn't touch that hand; not here, not in front of everybody.

She saw the second he recognized her, which really was just half a second after his hand—and his eyes and his cheekbones and his ears—forced her to admit the truth. She watched it cross his face: surprise, warmth, heat—definitely heat—before he cleared his throat and looked nothing but professional. Becky felt the blush all the way down to her toes, and if Will hadn't tossed the pom-pom pen on her desk, she would still be standing there, gawping like a guppy, while the new associate waited for her to return his handshake.

The new associate.

Oh God.

The new associate was a lawyer and a genius and had had a beard on Saturday night when he'd rocked her world several times over, and the look on his face told her that he remembered.

Becky wanted to crawl under her desk and die.

But she couldn't, not with a partner standing there.

She'd wait until the partner left. And he took his new legal genius with him. Then Becky could die.

Dammit, why had she sworn off lawyers?

Of all the libraries in all the world, Becky had walked into this one. Well, *he'd* walked into it. Becky was sitting behind a desk next to a floppy-haired hipster who was seriously pushing the firm's dress code.

That didn't matter. All that mattered was that he'd found her. He wouldn't have to search every crappy sports bar in Denver looking for her. Even better, he hadn't imagined her. That was the worst part, waking up in the morning, alone, thinking he'd made up the best sex of his life. But there was no way he could have conjured up Becky. She was too . . . he'd just never dreamed someone who looked like her would be as aggressive as she was. And he wasn't into, like, *Fifty Shades* stuff, but when she'd climbed on top of him and trapped his wrists above his head . . .

"And that's how you check your voice mail."

Kevin, the secretary for his division, looked at Foster expectantly. Foster wasn't sure what he expected. Acknowledgment that he'd understood the incredibly detailed instructions on an incredibly simple phone system? Well, he hadn't really been listening. But how hard could voice mail be?

"Thanks, that's great," he said, giving Kevin an acknowledging nod.

"Anything else you need, supplies, whatever, just let me know. I can get into the supply closet."

Kevin jangled the keys hanging from around his neck. "I'm the only one with a key to the supply closet."

"Oh."

"Not even the senior partners have one," Kevin said, with what could only be described as glee.

"You're the man for office supplies, got it."

"Some of the other admins have a key, but I'm responsible for the supplies for this division. You want pens, you ask me."

"OK."

"Legal pads, ask me."

"Stapler?"

"You've already got one. I planned ahead." Kevin pointed at the top drawer of his desk, which Foster had been too busy to open. He did so now, and what do you know, a shiny new stapler. And scissors. And a letter opener.

"Wow, looks like you thought of everything."

"If I didn't think of it, you probably don't need it. But if you do . . ." He jangled his keys again.

Foster took small comfort in the fact that, even outside of the prestigious-beyond-all-reason law firms in New York he was familiar with, there were little eccentricities in every law firm. In every office, probably. In fact, he was sure this wasn't unique to law firms, but there was something particular about the tension between lawyers and nonlawyers, everyone on their own little power trips between divisions and coworkers. That particular thing was animosity. Foster hated political crap. He just wanted to figure stuff out and write briefs about it.

That was probably oversimplifying it.

But really, he could simplify it even more.

He just wanted to win.

And maybe sleep with Becky again.

He knew she had recognized him. Women didn't turn red and stammery like that just over his good looks, no matter how much he liked to pretend they did.

He'd have to figure out a way to talk to her again. He'd probably need a lot of research help on this case. Usually, he sent one of the junior associates down to work with the librarian, but maybe that wasn't how things worked at P&G. Or, if it was, there was no reason he had to work like that. There was no reason he couldn't take a hands-on approach to the research.

Which was exactly what he didn't need to do. Not only because, hello, unprofessional to bill a client because you wanted to flirt with a librarian. It wouldn't be the shadiest thing a law firm had ever done, but he had ethics. For the moment. As long as he didn't think about the way her hair had cascaded around their faces, then brushed down his chest and his abdomen . . .

No. Definitely not.

Besides which, he had enough work of his own on this case without also doing the work he could delegate. P&G had hired him to win this business with Goliath, and now that he was here, he really needed to prove himself. Not that he couldn't win the case—he'd won stickier intellectual property cases before—but if he was going to leverage this victory for whatever his next move was going to be, he needed this to go perfectly. That meant junior associates who were as hungry as he was, and definitely no distractions from the hot librarian.

At least no distractions when he could be working. During off-hours . . .

And hadn't Madison accused him of turning into their workaholic father? So maybe Becky wouldn't be a distraction. Maybe she'd be the key to his finally learning what all this work-life balance nonsense was all about.

As if summoned by the inner gods of delegation, a clerk—Claire, maybe? He really had to learn people's names—wheeled a dolly full of Bankers Boxes past his office.

Ah, the Goliath case. The case that would move his reputation from up-and-coming intellectual property whiz kid to an IP expert who could write his own ticket anywhere. All his colleagues in New York had said he was crazy to move to a smaller market. Even if he made partner in Denver, it was nowhere near as prestigious as making partner in New York. But P&G had a relationship with Goliath, and Goliath had the IP case of the century. Throw in one New York IP expert and there was no way P&G couldn't win the business, no way Goliath could lose.

Foster had done his due diligence. He'd cut his teeth working on a big case for Monsanto, and he knew what it took to win a case that crossed patent law with intellectual property law and the business of corporate secrets and scientific inquiry. And this case had it all.

Goliath had developed an herbicide that killed invasive species and was making them a ton of money in the home gardening market. But it turned out that while killing invasive species, the herbicide was also poisoning native pollinators, which meant native species didn't stand a chance. So they'd pulled the product.

Now CoLabs, also based outside of Denver, was bringing to market an herbicide that would attack invasive species but leave the bees alone. Bees were all over the news right now—or at least bees' place in the ecosystem and the importance of not just letting them die off was. This product was going to mean a ton of business.

Except the origin of their herbicide was Goliath's. So Goliath was suing. Without their bee-killing herbicide, CoLabs wouldn't have their bee saver. So Goliath was going to win.

Just thinking about it made his fingers twitch. In

a good way. The case was complicated, relying on layers and layers of balancing previous case law in both the medical and business fields. Hence the boxes and boxes of files. And they weren't even done with the discovery phase. Bees were hot right now, too, and it seemed like every day there were more news stories, more peer-reviewed studies, more *more* to go through to get to the heart of the case. If only he knew of a librarian who could help him keep track . . .

No time to think about Becky. He had a conference room full of boxes to go through, interns to do the grunt work, and, most importantly, he had a case to win.

Chapter Six

"It's him! Foster Deacon is him," Becky whispered violently into her phone.

"What? Foster who is who? Are you in a tunnel?" Dakota's voice sounded only a little alarmed, which, for Dakota, was a lot.

"I'm in the bathroom," Becky told her.

"Gross."

"I'm not going to the bathroom. I'm just . . . hold on." She listened to what sounded like the door opening. She poked her head out of the stall. "False alarm."

"Beck, what's going on? Can't you go somewhere private?"

"No! Yes. The bathroom is private. Ack, I don't know."

"Can you meet me for coffee?"

"Yes. But not right now. I'm on reference duty."

"But you're in the bathroom."

"We're allowed to take bathroom breaks."

"So just tell me what's wrong! You're making me nervous."

"I can't. Hold on." Becky listened again, just to make sure she was still alone. She stepped out of the stall and leaned down to peek under each stall.

"Becky!"

"I'm back. OK, are you listening?"

"Beck, I've been listening for the past five minutes. You just haven't actually said anything except that there's a massive crisis."

"OK, listen. Remember that new hotshot IP guy starting at P&G?"

"I only understood like three of those words."

"A new lawyer."

"OK, you didn't tell me. Or you did and I didn't care. Doesn't matter. I understand now. There's a new lawyer at work. Don't tell me you're in love with him."

"He's the lumberjack."

Silence on the other end of the line.

"Dakota?"

"Get out of there now."

"I can't! I'm on reference."

"You need to quit your job."

"What? No!"

"There's no other way. Becky, with such close proximity, you can't *not* fall in love with him."

"I'm not worried about that," Becky said, incredulous. "I'm off lawyers. And anyway, even if I wasn't, I wouldn't go for him. He's a genius."

Silence again.

"D?"

"How do you know he's a genius? And why won't you fall in love with one?"

"Because geniuses make for terrible families, and I want a nice, normal family life."

"Oh, Beck."

"No, this is good. Because the no-lawyer thing is new, so it might be easier to break my rule. But the no-geniuses thing, that's, like, carved in stone. So there's no way I can fall in love."

"Okaaay. So why are you calling me in a panic?"

Becky took a deep breath. "I'm not sure exactly. I just freaked out. I'm OK now. It'll just be a little awkward for a while. Then it will be fine. Then we can forget it and I'll meet a real lumberjack. Or— do you know any pirates?"

"Are you drunk?"

"What? No, I'm at work!"

"That guy Will didn't give you a pill or something, did he?"

"No! He's not a drug dealer. He's just lazy."

"And he's not a genius. Maybe you should get with him."

Becky snorted.

"Oh, hey, that reminds me . . ." Dakota trailed off without telling her what reminded her of what.

"D?"

The door opened, and this time someone did come in. Linda from HR, who gave Becky a funny look.

Fair enough.

"OK, real quick," Dakota said in a rush. "They announced the MacArthur Fellowships today and I looked at the list just for the heck of it, and your sister is on it."

"What?"

"Your sister. Miranda? She's a genius."

Becky felt her face get hot like it did whenever anyone mentioned any member of her family. Not that there were any issues there or anything.

"I know she's a genius."

"No, like, officially. The MacArthur Genius Grant?"

"Right." Sure, she knew all about those. Recipients got a large amount of money to do with whatever they pleased as a reward for being supergood at something. Lin-Manuel Miranda got one.

And her sister.

Becky heard Linda cough from inside the stall. Probably she'd spent enough time on the phone in the bathroom.

"You okay, Becky?"

"Yeah, sure. I gotta go. Thanks for telling me," she said, even though she didn't really mean it. I mean, it wasn't *bad* to know, but it didn't really have anything to do with her life. It wasn't like her sister would have told her. Or anyone in her family.

Her family was real tight like that.

Becky hung up, then washed her hands just for the hell of it.

As she clopped down the hallway back to her office, her pants digging into her waist, she thought about her sister the genius. Both of her sisters were geniuses, really. Miranda was a molecular biologist and Astrid was an astrophysicist. Her parents, too, were lauded research scientists working at CU Boulder.

Whereas Becky was just a librarian.

Not just a librarian, dammit. Her work was interesting and important, and it was library science, dammit!

Try telling her family that. Ah, yes, she had. Many times.

There were only so many pitying gazes a girl could take before she stopped trying to organize her family of geniuses into a normal family get-together. Christmas was a nuisance because all the labs were closed, so they spent their time catching up on professional reading. Birthdays, forget it. She doubted her parents knew their own birthdays, let alone their daughters'. How about a nice Sunday night meal? But why would we spend all that time cooking when we can just eat something quick and get back to work?

That was why Becky wanted a normal life. Normal people didn't spend all their time stressing about the viability of samples and arguing over the efficacies of different research methodologies. At least they didn't always do that. They talked about books and watched movies and sometimes just did nothing but enjoy one another's company. They didn't spend the limited time they had together comparing fellowships and undermining the value of someone with just an above-average intellect.

That's what Dakota didn't understand. Her family was eccentric, but they were eccentric in a tree-hugger kind of way. Her dad wore socks with his Birkenstocks, but he still loved his kids and told them so with regularity. They were against organized religion and also the commercialization of religious holidays, but they still gathered together to share family meals.

Even Dakota's weird family was so normal compared to hers. She thought Becky's dreams were boring, but for Becky, a white picket fence was the most transgressive thing she could achieve.

That's all she'd wanted. A normal job, a nice house, a dog, and a nongenius lumberjack. Was that so much to ask for?

For now, she'd have to settle on the normal job. She walked back into the library, glad to see that Will had moved on to his next distraction for the afternoon. It was just about lunchtime, too, so she would have the whole library to herself to answer email requests and, if she was really lucky, do a little cataloging. Not entirely thrilling, but enough to keep her distracted from her woefully pathetic life. Because it wasn't woefully pathetic. It was great. It was fine. It wasn't there yet, but it was going places. She was just a little off-balance, that was all. A productive afternoon would get her back on track, she thought.

Until she walked past the reference desk and saw Foster there, waiting.

Waiting for her.

* * *

He wasn't stalking her.

Even though the fact that he had to tell himself that he wasn't stalking her was probably an indication that he was getting close.

But she was the librarian on duty and he needed help. Fine, so he could have sent one of the associates down here, or even one of the clerks. But he was having a problem delegating. This was a big case. It needed to be done right.

"Hello, Mr. Deacon," she said as she scooted behind the desk.

"Seriously?"

"Seriously what?"

"You don't have to call me Mr. Deacon. You've seen me naked."

Her eyes widened and she swung her head around. But no, they were alone. He wouldn't have said that if there was anyone else to hear.

Hmm . . . maybe that was a sign he shouldn't be saying that to her.

Pfft.

"I mean, just call me Foster."

"Not Deke?"

"Ugh, please, no. That's a college nickname."

"Then why didn't you correct me?"

When they were getting all sweaty and naked, she meant. He should have. He'd thought about it. But, well. "I was distracted."

He smiled at her, remembering how sweet those distractions were.

She rolled her eyes.

OK. Not what he was expecting.

"What can I do for you, Foster?"

"Have lunch with me?"

She looked surprised. "Why?"

"Um. Because I like you? And I think you like me, too?"

"Is that why you came down here, to ask me out?"

"No. I mean, partly." God, he was getting all discombobulated. Madison would be laughing her head off if she could see him. "I came down here because I need you to look into a few things for me."

"Good."

"But also to ask you out."

"How about if you tell me your reference needs?"

She blushed when she said *needs*.

He knew she liked him.

But he did have reference needs. First, reference. Then, flirting.

"I'm looking for cases that involve the transfer of intellectual property rights from research institutions to anywhere outside of that institution. Individual scientists, corporations, all that."

"OK." She started typing. He watched her fingers fly. He thought about intellectual property rights. "Is there a specific field of science you want me to focus on?"

"No. I'm casting a pretty broad net to start with. I've got some that were tried in New York courts;

would it help if I sent them to you? To see if there's anything similar in Colorado?"

"Yes. So we're just looking in Colorado? Federal?"

"Yes. But so far, Colorado is the only state. Well . . ." He thought about Goliath and where its major research institutions were. "Wyoming too." He didn't think the case would be relevant to the work they were doing in Wyoming, but better to be prepared. "And California," he added, remembering more details. "And . . . that's probably it."

"You know, most people just send an email. You know, so they have time to turn their thoughts into an actual query?"

"Is this too much?"

She looked offended. Although, to be fair, he had sort of meant to offend her.

"No. But it will save us both—and the client, I'm assuming?—a lot of time and money if I could have all the information before I begin."

"That's very conscientious of you."

"Thank you. Deadline?"

"ASAP."

"Of course. You can't get more specific than that?"

"Tomorrow afternoon."

"Great. Anything else?"

"Have lunch with me."

"No."

Well, that was the second time he'd asked her. And the first time she'd said no, technically. But he wasn't going to beg.

"Not even to thank you for your hard work?"

She stood up. He took a step back.

"I get a salary, Foster, so no other thanks are necessary. I'd really appreciate it if we could keep our relationship professional."

"OK. Got it."

"So don't come down here reminding me of . . ." She trailed off and blushed again. Ha, like he needed to remind her.

But she'd said no. "I'll send an associate down to get whatever you come up with."

"Or I'll put it in the mail."

"Not sure if I trust Will with that."

"You've only been here a day," she said with a little bit of a laugh. "How can you possibly know who's not trustworthy?"

"Genius," he said, tapping his temple.

The laugh died on her lips. She sat down and started typing.

Foster knew when he was dismissed. So he left.

Good. He didn't care. This case was going to make or break his career and an office entanglement would only make things more . . . entangled. So even though she got to it first, it was right that they didn't see each other socially.

Good.

That was good.

Totally good.

He walked right past his office and would have kept going if Kevin hadn't stopped him to tell him he had a phone call.

"Should I tell them you're at lunch?"

"No, put them through."

"You're sure? You seem kind of . . . out of it."

"You've known me one day. Put the call through."

"OK." Kevin pouted as he pressed numbers on the phone. "Then I'm ordering you a damn sandwich."

To: Rebecca Schrader
From: Foster Deacon
Subject: Journal Subscriptions

Hi Becky,

Please find attached a list of journals P&G does not currently subscribe to.

Thank you for addressing this oversight.

Foster

To: Foster Deacon
From: Rebecca Schrader
Subject: Re: Journal Subscriptions

Hi Foster,

Thank you for your suggestion. This is not an oversight. We have access to a full three-quarters of this list through HeinOnline. Feel free to make an appointment with another librarian if you need assistance navigating this resource. I recently designed a training for your junior associates and they seemed to find it helpful; perhaps they can assist.

Becky

To: Rebecca Schrader
From: Foster Deacon
Subject: Re: Re: Journal Subscriptions

Becky,

Thank you for your quick response. I am very familiar with HeinOnline, having gone to actual law school. The three-quarters of the journals available through this database have a floating wall. I need the most current issues. I also need access to the more than one-quarter of the journals that are not covered in HeinOnline.

Thank you for reconsidering.

Foster

To: Foster Deacon
From: Rebecca Schrader
Subject: Re: Re: Re: Journal Subscriptions

Foster—

As a professional law librarian, I can assure you that I am aware of the contents of each of these journals. If you have a specific research question, I would be happy to refer you to one of the other librarians.

—Becky

To: Rebecca Schrader
From: Foster Deacon
Subject: Re: Re: Re: Re: Journal Subscriptions

Becky—

I'm sorry, I must have misunderstood the role of the library in this firm. In New York, the library had a budget reserved for purchasing materials necessary to the case law being practiced.

Please let me know if you prefer to handle things differently.

Foster

To: Foster Deacon
From: Rebecca Schrader
Subject: Re: Re: Re: Re: Re: Journal Subscriptions

Foster—

The law library at P&G, like law libraries at all corporate law firms, does indeed have a materials budget. I'd be happy to refer you to the director for more information.

B

To: Rebecca Schrader
From: Foster Deacon
Subject: Re: Re: Re: Re: Re: Re: Journal Subscriptions

Becky,

What is this about? I understand that you don't want to go out with me and I've respected your boundaries. I don't see what I've done to deserve this unprofessional treatment.

To: Rebecca Schrader
From: Foster Deacon
Subject: Re: Re: Re: Re: Re: Re: Journal Subscriptions

Becky—

Why aren't you responding? You can't ignore me. This is a real work request!

To: Rebecca Schrader
From: Foster Deacon
Subject: Re: Re: Re: Re: Re: Re: Journal Subscriptions

Becky—

I wasn't going to also ask you out for a drink because it's Friday night. That's fine; you've gone home. See if I care.

<<Microsoft Outlook has recalled the last three messages>>

Chapter Seven

Foster was on shelter pickup duty again.

Because he was a caring older brother, he was even going early. Madison said they always needed people to walk the dogs, get them used to leashes, and give them some exercise. He could use a good, long walk. It had been a stressful first week of work and he needed time away from the office—and the librarian—to clear his head so he could head into next week ready to fight.

For his client. Not fight the librarian.

Why would he even fight the librarian?

Just because he kind of liked arguing with her.

Even though she wouldn't agree to order those journals he needed.

And, fine, he'd pulled one of the junior associates away from document review to look up a few things and it turned out, Becky was right, he didn't *need* all those specific journals all the time.

He didn't like being wrong.

He needed a walk.

Or a run. Maybe there was a dog who'd want to run. He could go for that kind of dog, actually. Maybe he'd be open to adopting a running dog, if it seemed like the kind of dog Madison could take care of when he went back to New York. And it'd make Madison happy. So that felt like a win-win.

His phone rang and he pressed the button on his steering wheel to pick up the call with Bluetooth.

"Hi, Mom."

"Don't forget to pick up your sister today, sweetheart."

"I'm on the way now."

"What? No! She's not done until five. If you pick her up early, she'll miss out on community service hours and then—"

"Mom. Relax. I told her I'd come early to help out."

"Don't they have people to do that?"

"Yes. And today I'm going to be one of those people."

"You always were so generous with your time."

He was? He didn't remember being very volunteer-oriented. In fact, he couldn't remember the last time he'd done something that wasn't for work or for socializing.

Well, he'd had vigorous sex with Becky.

But that was a week ago and was clearly never to be repeated. Which was fine.

"What are your plans for this evening?"

Oh, right. He was talking to his mother.

"Nothing. I was going to see if Madison wanted to check out a movie or something."

"Oh, good. Yes, keep her out of the house."

"You're not having positive communication?"

"We are, if you mean she responds with the bare minimum of grunts when I ask her a question. Honestly. I understand it's hard to be a teenager, but that's no excuse to lose one's manners."

"OK, Mom."

"And I spoke to Mrs. Collins, who said the Kendalls are going out of town, and last time that happened, well . . ."

"Well what?"

"Honestly, Foster. That was the night Madison went to the party and those awful children pressured her to drink."

"Was that how it happened?" Knowing Madison, Foster was pretty sure the truth was a little different from the way his mother saw it. And, most likely, from the way Madison told it.

"Anyway, take good care of her tonight. Oh, speaking of Mrs. Collins, you know who's back in town?"

"Mr. Collins?"

"Francesca! I told her that you were in town working on a big case and she seemed very excited. I'll text you her number—you can take her out."

"Uh." He remembered Franny Collins. She was a year or two younger than he, and she was always hanging around the events his mother dragged him to. And for a while there, she was always showing up at his lacrosse games. Then . . .

"Didn't she get married?" In fact, Foster was pretty sure he was at the wedding.

"Oh, that's all old news. The husband was hugely

unacceptable. We never wish heartache on our children, but Mrs. Collins is so relieved."

"Well, I'm gonna be pretty busy with this case." He was sure Franny Collins was a perfectly lovely person. He just had no interest in rediscovering that. "You know how it is." He tried applying some of his mother's patented guilt trip. Because she did know; she was married to a lawyer who worked even crazier hours than Foster did and who never had time for anything but work.

"All work and no play, Foster."

"I'm playing, Mom. I'm going to walk some dogs right now, in fact."

"Well, if you have time to walk wild shelter dogs, you have time to take Francesca Collins out to dinner."

"I don't, actually."

"How about if I call her and set up . . ."

"Gotta go, Mom. I'm here. See you when I drop Madison off later."

"But just one—"

He shouldn't have done it; he knew that. But he did anyway. He hung up on his mother.

Maybe it wouldn't be so bad, one date with Franny Collins. He really wasn't doing anything else. He definitely wasn't dating a librarian.

Not that he wouldn't date a librarian. It wasn't like Becky worked for him, specifically. It just seemed . . . complicated. Whenever anyone dated in the office, it got complicated. Even if the relationship worked out, even if it ended in marriage—which didn't always mean it worked out, just that it reached its inevitable conclusion—there was still too much potential for complication. He didn't want complicated.

There was no ethical reason why he couldn't date her. It wasn't like she reported to him. He hated those guys who preyed on the legal secretaries and junior associates. This wouldn't be that. They weren't equals, exactly. Just   coworkers. In different departments. He could go weeks without seeing her around the office, potentially. If he wanted to avoid her, he totally could.

And she could totally avoid him. Which was what she had been doing. No, that was reading too much into it. Their paths just hadn't crossed. True, he'd been to the library quite a few times in the past few days, way more than he ever usually needed to go. He just wanted to make his requests in person. While he got to know people. Even though it was way more convenient for them to get the requests by email, apparently. It was just that whenever he went to the library, Becky wasn't there.

Not that he was going to see her.

Jesus, sooner or later he was going to have to admit he'd been rejected.

But that hurt his ego. And it was a sunny Saturday afternoon, and who knew when it would be this sunny and warm again? So there was no reason for him to have to face anything, at least until Monday. And on Monday he could avoid the library, which shouldn't be hard because, as Becky had so helpfully pointed out, he could send one of the juniors to the library for him. Or contact the library electronically.

Or he could just go in when Becky wasn't there, which was apparently whenever he was, so that shouldn't be hard.

Or he could quit mooning over a woman who, despite their mind-blowing connection, wasn't interested in him.

He parked next to a little blue compact car and dropped his head onto the steering wheel. He had to get it together. He had moved back home to win a career-making case and to make sure Madison didn't totally embrace a life of crime. He hadn't moved here for romantic complications. And right now, a date with Franny Collins felt a hell of a lot less complicated than whatever he was doing with Becky.

Before he gave in to the crazy urge to call Franny—because there was no way that would be uncomplicated—he reminded himself that he was here to pick up his sister from her court-ordered community service and take her to dinner, where he could give her a stern talking-to about listening to their mother and maybe getting better grades. Which would go over great. Because when he was a teenager, he definitely listened to Lydia and focused on nothing but school and being a good son.

Ha. Still, his kind of trouble was harmless. And virtually any bad thing he did that caused him to get in trouble with any sort of authority was always in pursuit of a girl.

He always got the girl.

Unless the girl was Becky.

Pull it together, Foster, he told himself, not that he would listen.

He got out of the car and went to find his baby sister.

"See? He's an asshole. You don't have to worry about him anymore."

Becky chewed on her lower lip and shifted her camera bag. Dakota was right. It seemed Dakota was always right, at least when it came to men.

Well, most men. She did notice Bullhorn was hanging around a lot.

Not that Bullhorn wasn't a perfectly nice guy. And he seemed totally smitten with Dakota. Becky would have been worried for the poor guy if she hadn't seen Dakota sneaking looks at him when he wasn't watching.

They'd just waved him off for a walk with three retriever mixes, bonded siblings who'd come in together and, hopefully, would leave together. Becky would shoot them later today, if Bullhorn didn't get them too muddy.

The wait between photo shoots gave Becky just enough time to tell Dakota that, yes, Foster was Deke the Lumberjack, and no, there was no way that was happening. In addition to being a lawyer (no) and a genius (heck no), he was also a pompous jerk, which didn't necessarily go with the lawyer and the genius part, but it sure wasn't helping break down any stereotypes.

He did look good in his suits, though.

And she knew he looked good out of them.

But he looked different without the beard. He definitely didn't look bad—it was practically a crime to cover up that jaw—but he didn't look like Deke. He looked like Foster, Deke's less-rugged, jerkier twin brother.

Oh, that was a thought. What if Foster really had a secret twin brother? And they were separated at birth? And Becky would go out one night and see that gorgeous face with that delicious beard and it would be . . .

"Hello! Earth to Becky!"

Dakota's amused shout woke Becky out of her fantasy. And good thing—secret twins? She was spending way too much time . . . well, she didn't know what she was spending way too much time doing. Thinking about Foster, probably.

For example, the guy who was standing in the doorway to the shelter looked just like him.

She blinked.

Nope, that was Foster.

"What are you doing here?" she asked in a voice that sounded more angry than politely surprised.

"Becky?" he said, and he sounded pissed, too.

Dakota cleared her throat. "Hi. Deke, right?" Becky rolled her eyes. Dakota knew very well that it wasn't Deke, and the gleam in Dakota's eyes told Becky she knew it.

"Actually, it's Foster."

"Oh, didn't you introduce yourself as Deke at the bar?" Dakota's face was pure innocence.

Becky wanted to vomit.

Foster rubbed the back of his neck. "Yeah. Sorry about that. I already apologized to Becky."

"Oh, I don't think you have anything to apologize to Becky about."

Becky didn't think she'd ever seen a man blush before. It made her want to take out her camera and shoot.

Yes, she reminded herself. She wanted to shoot Foster.

Or punch him.

Or at least just stop running into him.

That would make it so much easier to ignore him and his smell. If he just wouldn't be here, she wouldn't be tempted to lean into him and inhale along the pulse in his neck. Then she wouldn't have to remember how much she liked that, and how much that made him shiver and how that made him—

"Becky!"

"Huh?" Not thinking about that at all, she reminded herself.

"Foster was just explaining that he's here to pick up his sister."

"Sister?"

"Yeah. She told me she was working with a photographer named Becky. Is that you?"

"No, it's our other photographer named Becky," Dakota said, not that either of them was paying attention.

"Maddie's your sister?"

"I thought you were a librarian?"

"And I thought Maddie was working until five today," Dakota interrupted.

"Oh, she is," Foster explained. "I came here to walk dogs."

"Oh, you just missed Bullhorn."

"Bullhorn is here walking dogs?"

"He started volunteering. He's very helpful."

"Is Franny Collins here, too?"

"Is that a dog?"

"Never mind. So, Becky. Wow. A librarian *and* a photographer."

"I know, it's like a person can have different facets to her personality or something." For example, Foster was an attentive and athletic lover and he was also a condescending asshole.

"Is Madison around? I'd like to tell her I'm here."

To get your stupid big-brother points. Gah, she couldn't believe this was the older brother Maddie was all gaga about.

"She's in the puppy room," Dakota said. "I'll go get her."

"I'll come with you," Becky said.

Foster followed, uninvited.

She was going to turn around and tell Foster that he didn't need to follow her around, that they were perfectly capable of finding Maddie without him, but when she got to the puppy room, she forgot all about Foster.

Maddie was sitting cross-legged in the middle of the floor with poor old Starr cradled in her arms. And Maddie was further damaging Starr's fur by crying into it.

"What's wrong?" Foster pushed past them and got down on the floor next to his sister.

"Th-th-this is Starr," Maddie hiccupped.

"OK," he said, pushing her bangs out of her face. "Hi, Starr."

"I love her."

"Oh. Wow. Um. Is Starr a dog?"

"Sweetie," Dakota interrupted, "you're not supposed to take the dogs out of their cages without an employee in here."

"But Starr looked so sad and scared back there, and then when I picked her up, she stopped shaking and cuddled right into me and I love her."

Foster looked at Becky, panicked. But Becky could do nothing to help him. She loved Starr, too. Dirty little ball of mats that she was.

Fortunately, Dakota, who was right about everything, was there.

"I know you do," she said, gently peeling Starr out of Maddie's arms. Starr gave a panicked wiggle and Dakota almost lost her, but then the dog settled into her shoulder and seemed to calm down immediately. "God, I know it. But that's the thing about working here. You fall in love with all of them. And that's good."

"It doesn't feel good."

Dakota laughed a little. "But doesn't it make you feel like the work you're doing here is important?"

Maddie wiped her eyes. "Yeah. I'm so glad I got drunk and got caught."

Foster made a choking sound.

"I'm just kidding, doofus."

"I know, stinker." He pulled her in to him and kissed the top of her head. "Now, I came here to walk some dogs. Do you have any life-size ones who need some exercise?" He stood up and stretched out his hands to his sister. She let him pull her up and then fell into his arms.

Great, now Becky was going to have to like him.

"Do you want to help with the photos?" Maddie asked him.

"Sure. I mean, if it's OK with Becky." He looked over Maddie's head at Becky, and like she could say no to that.

"No problem."

No problem at all.

"Hamilton! Over here, Hamilton!"

Foster watched as Madison squeaked a toy behind Becky's ear, but it was no use. Hamilton the Hound was way more interested in sniffing the grass around him than he was in looking photo fabulous for the shelter's Facebook page. While they got set up—which mostly involved Maddie running around with Hamilton to tire him out a little bit—he'd pulled out his phone and scrolled through to look at some of Becky's work.

He didn't know what a good dog portrait looked like, but all the dogs looked friendly and cute, with individual personalities on display—curious, happy, adoring—so he guessed Becky was pretty good at it. And once they started, he liked watching her work. She got down on the dog's level, made all kinds of goofy noises while she snapped pictures. And when Hamilton jumped on her to give her a kiss, she went down laughing.

God, she had a great laugh.

"Hamilton! Hammy!"

Becky pointed and gave some quiet instructions to Madison, who actually listened without arguing.

There was clearly something magical about Becky.

Madison stepped out from behind Becky and the camera and continued to squeak.

Hamilton looked up at them, then back at the grass.

"Maybe he's not into squeaks," Madison suggested. "It is pretty annoying."

"That's all I've got. I used up all my treats." They'd used the last of them to get Lily, a giantess who definitely had some Great Pyrenees in her, to submit to a brushing. It was worth it; the shots came out great, or at least it seemed that way in the cursory glance Becky gave them while Madison picked another dog to photograph. Unfortunately, that left them treatless with Hamilton. He was easy enough to persuade to come outside. It was getting him to look at them that was proving to be difficult.

"He's looking at me!" Madison whispered, freezing in place.

Becky snapped a shot. Hamilton looked at her. Sort of. His head was still pointed grassward, but his eyes were following Madison.

That was a pretty cute dog. Not a running partner—not if he was that obsessed with grass—but Foster could imagine him with a family full of kids, tearing around in a gloriously grassy yard.

"What are you smiling at?" Madison asked him as she came up to the fence with Hamilton's leash in tow.

"Nothing." He definitely wasn't smiling at the idea of a big yard and a big family. Yikes. "You guys did good out there."

"We're not done yet. Move." She pushed the gate a little, and he got out of the way so she could open it. Hamilton stopped to receive a scratch behind his ears and then Maddie ran with him back inside.

Becky was sitting on the grass inside the fenced enclosure, leaning over her camera to shield it from the sun. "Get any good shots?" he called out to her.

She looked up, as if she was surprised to see him still there. Her hair had come loose from her ponytail—that was Hamilton's fault—and she had a smudge of dirt on her cheek—also Hamilton. Before Foster knew what he was doing, he had opened the gate and was sitting next to her on the grass.

She narrowed her eyes at him. "What are you doing?"

"Just sitting." She gave him a suspicious look that was much less innocently curious than the dogs'. "I thought maybe we could have a conversation. You know, like humans."

"You're probably sitting in dog pee."

He took a deep breath. As much as he liked arguing with her, this was starting to get silly. It was a beautiful day, the sun was warming his back, and his sister was happy. "Can we start over?"

"What do you mean?"

"I mean, I think we got off on the wrong foot."

"No, I think we got off on a pretty amazing foot."

She blushed. Ha.

"I mean at work. And now here. I mean, I get it if you don't like me"—no, he didn't—"but I don't think that's true."

"Oh you don't, don't you?"

"I don't. I know it's not true for me."

She looked at him for a long moment. He could see the wheels turning in her head. "It's not true for me either," she said softly.

He felt a goofball smile spread across his face.

Becky smiled back.

"So," he said, leaning back into the grass. "How'd you end up here?"

"In Denver?"

"No, here." He waved his hand around them.

"In a fenced-in enclosure with a man who just talked me out of ambivalence?"

He sat up enough so he could see her face. She threw a piece of grass at him.

"Well, Dakota works here. She's the director. And I've always liked photography, but I never really did anything with it, you know? It was just sort of a hobby."

"Are you good?"

"Psh," she said, but then she paused. "Yeah. I'm OK."

"And Dakota convinced you to use your powers for good?"

"She's very persuasive."

"I'm starting to get that. I heard Bullhorn was here, too."

"Yeah. He's been gone a little while. I wonder if we should send out a search party."

"Nah. Bullhorn may be a loud goofball, but he's got an amazing sense of direction."

They sat together in the sun, him squinting up at the sky, her pulling up pieces of grass. Eventually, she lay back, too, so they were side by side, squinting together.

"So how did you get here?"

"Not the fenced-in enclosure here?"

"Denver here."

"I grew up here."

"Ah. Your family still around?"

"Sure."

"You don't sound very convinced of that."

"My family and I . . . we're not close."

"Ah. I feel like there's a story there."

She shrugged. "Not really. They're all really busy doing important, lifesaving work. I'm a librarian."

"You say that like being a librarian isn't lifesaving work."

"It's not. Not what I do."

"Are you saying P&G isn't practicing lifesaving law?"

"You're the legal genius, you tell me."

He thought about it. "I guess that depends on how you define life. And saving."

"Ha. Spoken like a true lawyer."

"So what kind of lifesaving work do your parents do?"

"They're both medical researchers. My sister is, too. Well, one of them. The other one is in space."

"What?"

"Yeah. She's an astrophysicist. She lives on the International Space Station."

"Wow."

"Yes. She's literally way above me. And my other sister, the medical researcher, just got a MacArthur Fellowship."

"Is that the Genius Grant?"

"Mm-hmm."

"Her and Lin-Manuel, huh?"

"Yup. All geniuses."

He put his hand on her knee. Not to get fresh, just to offer comfort. He knew what it was like to compete with members of your family; he'd rather die than admit it, but that was why he'd gone into law, to prove to his father that he could keep up. He couldn't imagine having that kind of competition with everyone in his family.

"So how come you took the job with P&G? I thought you were a hotshot in New York?"

"Hotshot? Where do you get your news from?"

"Will. He mostly gets it from Gert."

"Is Gert the eighty-year-old woman in documents?"

"Yup."

He took his hand back and tucked it behind his head. "I wouldn't say I was a hotshot." But that was only because he would never say the word *hotshot*. He'd been a big deal at his firm. He probably would have made partner in the next five years.

But then Madison got arrested and Mr. Polak,

who went to law school with his dad, called him about this business he was trying to win, and it wasn't New York, but he'd be near his sister. And he'd make partner in two years instead of five.

So yeah. He was kind of a big deal.

Which, he figured, would be exactly not what Becky wanted to hear.

But, what, he was supposed to make himself small so she would like him? That was some after-school special bullshit.

"It's OK, hotshot," she said. "I still like you."

Her eyes locked on his for the longest second of his life.

"I mean . . . I don't mean *like* you like you."

"You don't, huh?"

"Gosh, where are all those dogs we're supposed to photograph?" She put a hand on his chest and pushed him down. But just when he was about to grab her by the waist, she used the leverage to push herself up to a standing position.

She liked him.

That shouldn't make him so happy.

"Who's this one?" Becky called as soon as Maddie was even remotely within earshot. Not because she was desperate to get away from Foster. Because why would she want to get away from him? Just because they had magnetic chemistry and she had just admitted out loud that she liked him. Psh.

Too bad he was everything she didn't like in a

potential mate. If he was, she'd really like him. Like, like him like him.

"I tried to get Starr," Maddie said as she opened the gate and let their next victim in. As soon as she shut the gate and took the leash off, the dog made a beeline for Foster, still lying on the grass. Becky heard the *oof* as thirty pounds of exuberant canine made contact with Foster's midsection.

"This guy will be great. Good choice."

"It wasn't my choice." Maddie pouted. "Dakota wouldn't let me take Starr."

"Honey, if Dakota says Starr isn't ready, she's not ready."

"But if we don't shoot her, no one will adopt her, and if no one adopts her, she'll never get out of that cage."

Becky put a hand on Maddie's back. So the kid had feelings after all. "Maybe you could take her?" As soon as Becky said that, she knew she shouldn't have. If she had any doubts, she just had to look at the way Maddie's eyes lit up, then quickly dimmed.

"Your parents don't like dogs?" she asked, doing a terrible job of keeping her head down and minding her own business.

Maddie snorted. "My mother would never allow a dog like Starr into her house."

Becky knew the mother was a bit of a neat freak, which was why, she figured, Maddie always looked like a slob. She could appreciate that kind of act of rebellion. Or maybe Maddie just dressed the way the kids were dressing these days.

Well, she was now officially old. She and Starr would make a great couple.

"The form says she's housebroken."

"Anyway, my father would never want such a tiny dog. He'd want a big, manly dog. A purebred hunting dog."

"Your dad's a hunter?" Becky thought he was a big, fancy lawyer. Like Foster. Ugh.

"No, but he'd want the kind of dog that rich, manly people have."

Becky thought she understood what Maddie meant. Her own father would never dream of subscribing to such a traditional view of masculinity, and Becky had grown up understanding all about the toxicity of it and the ways society forced men to behave against their best interests . . . maybe *her* parents would want Starr.

No. Her parents could barely feed themselves. She couldn't put Starr through that. Looked like the poor girl had been through enough.

"Can't you talk to Dakota?" Maddie asked hopefully.

Ha. Like Becky could get Dakota to change her mind about anything. Like anyone could. Anyway, she was the expert in this situation, so as much as Becky wanted to intervene, there was no point.

Besides, there was no way Starr was ready for her close-up.

"Not today. But we'll get her camera ready, don't worry."

"I'm not worried," Maddie lied.

"Hey, are you guys doing something with this dog or are you just going to let him attack me?"

Becky turned to find Foster rolling around with the dog, letting himself be covered in kisses. He had grass in his hair.

Becky took a deep breath. *You don't like him like him,* she reminded herself.

"Tigger, come here!" The dog gave Foster one more quick lick, then trotted happily over to Maddie, his tongue lolling out of his smiling mouth.

"Tigger? Why is he called Tigger?" Becky asked. "He looks nothing like a Tigger." He was white with big black spots like a hound dog, but he had the face and ears of a boxer and the blue eyes of a cattle dog or a husky.

This was one interesting-looking dog.

Interesting dogs were good for business.

But still, he was no Tigger.

"Ready?" Maddie asked.

"Ready for what?"

"Foster, get out of the way," she called to her brother, and he got up and stood by them.

"Watch. Tigger, jump!" She started running across the yard.

And Tigger . . . well, it was clear how Tigger got his name.

She'd never seen a dog jump so high in her life.

"Oh my God!" Becky screamed with laughter as Tigger bounced his way across the yard in Maddie's wake. "Can you take a video of this?" she asked Foster, who'd been on his phone earlier—probably checking work email, the hotshot—so she knew he had the equipment.

He didn't say anything, so she took her eyes off Tigger for a second, only to see him with his phone out, covering his mouth and following the bouncy procession around the enclosure.

Becky stood back. A video would definitely make people fall in love with Tigger. And the more people who fell in love with him, the more likely he was to get adopted.

She tried not to think about Starr, sitting un-adoptable in her crate. Instead, she watched Tigger bounce, watched Maddie tire him out so he would sit still enough for her to take a photo that wasn't a complete bouncy blur, and she got to work.

Chapter Eight

Foster looked over at his sister in the front passenger seat, making crooning noises into the crate she refused to stow in the back.

"I know. My brother is a big meanie and won't let you out until we get home."

"Hey," he said. "That was Dakota's idea."

"I wasn't talking to you," Maddie said. "I was explaining it to Starr."

Foster sighed. How had he gotten himself into this situation?

Oh right. His kid sister was crying. Not the big, show-off tears she used to do when she didn't get her way. These were real, genuine tears of sadness and pity.

Or her temper-tantrum tears had gotten much more sophisticated.

And then Dakota had mentioned trying to find a foster family for Starr so she could come out of her shell, and Foster asked what that meant because he was an oblivious idiot who'd walked right into their trap.

Then he'd mentioned that maybe fostering Starr wouldn't be such a big deal because it was temporary, and Becky looked at him like he'd just peeled back his mask to reveal his secret superhero identity and Maddie jumped up and down and tackled him in a big hug, and then he was driving home with a can of wet kibble to last the night and a tiny dog that looked like an old mop.

He was a sucker.

It didn't help that Starr looked at him with those sad black eyes of hers. And he would never, even under pain of death, admit that that was what really sold him.

Besides, it was just temporary.

"We can take her to the groomer Dylan's mom goes to. They're used to dealing with ornery dogs."

"I don't think Starr is ornery," Foster said. And why, exactly, was he getting defensive about this temporary dog?

"I know, but they'll be gentle with her. You're gonna look so pretty when you're all cleaned up," Maddie said to the crate.

Starr let out a whimper. Foster tightened his grip on the wheel. That sad sound was stressing him out.

Fortunately, they were pulling into the parking garage under his building. As the three of them took the elevator up to his apartment, he mentally justified not clearing dog ownership—no, dog fostering—with Brock because Brock was out of the country and Starr's stay with him was only temporary.

"Can I spend the night? Just to make sure she's OK?"

Foster thought about being alone in his apartment with this quivering mop of nerves. "Yes. You can make sure she doesn't . . . I don't know, have a heart attack."

"That's not funny!"

"Well, it's not like she's going to tear the place up. How much damage can one little dog do?"

"And she has hardly any teeth. She'll be so good."

Because along with the fact that Starr wasn't even dog-size, Dakota had passed on the vet's report that she was in decent health, she was probably twelve years old, and most of her teeth had been removed. That was alarming, but Dakota reassured him that little dogs often had dental hygiene problems, and it was at least a good sign that the previous owner had paid attention to her health needs by removing rotting teeth that, if left alone, could cause much more damage.

Once they were inside, Maddie put the crate down in the middle of the living room and opened the gate.

"Aren't you going to take her out?" he asked when Maddie started to walk away.

"No. It's better if she gets acclimated and comes out when she feels comfortable."

Foster leaned down and peeked inside the crate. Starr was smooshed toward the back, but she watched him with curious eyes.

"Fine. When did you become such a dog expert?"

Maddie ignored him and started opening the

kitchen cabinets. "Where are your bowls? Never mind." She pulled out two small, plastic food storage containers, filled one with water, and emptied the can of wet food into the other.

"Make yourself at home," he muttered. He went in search of a clean set of sheets to make up the spare bed. "What do you want to do for dinner?" he called out. When she didn't answer, he went back down the hallway in search of an answer.

"Shh," Madison warned him as he entered the room. She was sitting on the corner of the couch. She'd turned the TV on low—that was fast—and was looking decidedly away from the crate.

"What's going—"

"Shh!"

He shhed, and watched a little moppy head peek out of the crate. Starr sniffed the carpet, then put out one tentative paw.

"Oh my God I'm going to die!" Maddie whispered. "She's so cute!"

Starr had two paws out, then three, then four. She looked around, taking in her new—temporary—home. And she barked.

"Yow." Foster rubbed his ear where he was pretty sure his eardrum was rupturing.

And that was apparently all Starr had to do to get her nervousness out of her system, because then she was wiggling and smiling—she was definitely smiling—and hopping all around, investigating every corner of the apartment before ending up in a full body wiggle at Madison's feet.

"Hi, baby, you want to come up?"

"No dogs on the sofa," he said as his sister picked up Starr and cuddled her. Well, the dog wasn't technically on the sofa. She was in Madison's arms on the sofa. Starr licked Madison's face and his sister giggled. "You have terrible breath," she said. "And I love you for it." Starr climbed out of her arms and onto the throw pillow at Madison's elbow. She walked in a few tight circles, then curled up in a ball and let out a contented sigh.

Technically, she was on a pillow and not on the sofa. So it was fine.

Anyway, it was only temporary.

Madison stretched out so her head was sharing the pillow with Starr. Starr gave her a lazy lick on the nose, then went to sleep.

Chapter Nine

Becky should feel grateful to Maddie and Starr and Dakota and even Foster, if she was being honest. The busy day at the shelter had taken her mind off the fact that tonight, she had a date with cruel, cruel fate.

Also known as dinner with her family.

When Becky was a kid, she'd spent way more energy than she cared to remember trying to corral her family of geniuses into the bare minimum of traditions of American life. But it was hard to share meals with people who only ate to sustain energy to stay up all night in the lab, and who thought any conversation that wasn't for the purpose of figuring out a sticky research problem was a waste of breath. And holidays, forget it. Not that Becky was religious, but it wouldn't have killed them to open a can of cranberries together when everyone had the day off anyway.

Despite their deceptive nuclearness—parents still married, three girls grown up into productive women—Becky still couldn't believe her parents had taken time away from work to go to the courthouse to get married, let alone procreate three times. But that was it. The only reason they had family photos was because Becky convinced them it would be interesting to document their growth. She should have given up long ago on trying to get her family to be anything even slightly smelling of normal. But, well, Betsy was stubborn. So it took way longer than it should have.

It took her all the way up until she started library school. She'd called her parents to let them know she'd been accepted, but they hadn't called back. After two weeks and her imagination getting the best of her—they'd probably been eaten by wild dogs!—she'd tracked down her mother at her lab. Her mom was annoyed at the interruption and even more annoyed when she learned Becky was just imparting information she already knew. *You could have called me back*, Becky said.

Why? To congratulate you on giving in to your inferior scientific proclivities?

So. That was her family.

She hadn't seen them in five years. Her parents had come to her graduation, but only because they were curious what a graduation ceremony was like, never having been to any of their own. (They weren't impressed.) The only reason she knew anything about any of her family was because Marley, Miranda's partner, was, relatively speaking, a softie. Plus, he had a much more junior position in Miranda's lab, so he had time to do silly things like tell Becky that her other sister was going into space.

She liked Marley, and she felt bad for him. She supposed if he didn't like the way Miranda barely seemed to acknowledge his existence, he wouldn't stay. He seemed to like being able to do his own thing. Still, she knew how difficult it was, herding the cats that were her parents and sisters, and she appreciated that he tried.

Tonight he only had to herd one sister, because Astrid was still on the ISS. How Marley had managed to get her parents and Miranda together at one table—at a restaurant, no less, where they would eat for the pleasure of eating—Becky had no idea.

And even though this was, on some level, what she'd always wanted, Becky was resentful that Marley had some kind of magic power she didn't. And she was nervous about how the evening would go. And, if she was really honest, she was a little bit excited to find out what a polite conversation with her family would be like.

Plus, she'd been reading about Razor's unique blend of American, Spanish, and Japanese cuisines and was dying to try it. So even if her family was a flop, at least the food would be good.

She hoped.

But you know what, she told herself as she walked into the restaurant, *even if it's terrible, you had a great afternoon. You took a round of adorable photos and Starr got out of the shelter.*

Because Foster took her.

God, outside of work, she really liked him.

She scanned the dimly lit seating area for her family. She didn't see them. But, sitting at the bar, talking to an animated brunette, was Foster.

If he wasn't looking so enthusiastic at having a drink with a woman who wasn't her, Becky would think he was stalking her. Good thing there was no reason for them to have drinks together; otherwise, she'd be really jealous right now. And if she was really jealous, she'd be able to justify the scenario that played out in her head, where she sauntered up to him, tapped him on the shoulder, and threw his beer in his pretty, clean shaven face.

Fortunately, she spotted her family right after that. And wasn't that telling, that being able to sneak past the bar unseen by Foster to enter the condescending bosom of her family was a relief?

She wondered if she would have felt differently if Foster was sitting at the bar alone.

No. No, definitely not.

Now, if he was sitting at the bar alone and had somehow miraculously grown back that sex beard, maybe.

Good thing he wasn't magic.

"Rebecca!" Marley was the only one who stood up as she approached the table. She returned his hug, then sat down to watch her family puzzle over the menu.

"I don't know what any of these things are," her father said.

"Hon, Rebecca's here," Marley said to Miranda.

Miranda leaned over to him and pointed at the menu. "What's this?"

"Wild rice?"

"I don't understand what's wild about it."

"Um. I don't know. Rebecca, do you know?"

"Marley, you can call me Becky. Everyone else does."

"Not everyone," her mother said.

Ah, so she wasn't invisible.

Marley gave her a sympathetic smile. Marley had a weird family, too. But his family was more along the lines of a Dakota-style family of charming eccentrics. His family were all musicians, and the ten kids in the family—ten!—were all named after artists their parents admired. Which was how Marley ended up with siblings named Ludwig, Patti, Neko, Fela, and Yo-Yo. She couldn't remember the rest of them. Marley was the only one who hadn't inherited a stitch of musicality, so he was the only one who didn't tour with the family band. So he knew a little bit about being the black sheep.

It was because she liked Marley so much that she was there. It was important for him to celebrate Miranda's achievements and he persisted in living under the delusion that her parents would acknowledge their pride out loud, and in public.

Of course they were here, in public, so maybe it wasn't a delusion. Maybe it was just a delusion when it came to Becky's achievements.

She briefly considered joining Foster and his new girlfriend at the bar.

But then Marley squeezed her shoulder and

thanked her for coming to celebrate Miranda, and she decided she wasn't that much of a jerk.

"Congratulations, Miranda," she said, ignoring her parents. For now anyway.

"Oh! Hi, Rebecca. Thanks."

"That must have been a surprise, huh? Getting that phone call?"

Miranda shrugged. She was confident enough in her genius to know it would someday be recognized. "I'll get really excited when it's the Nobel committee."

"That's your problem, Miranda. You never aim high enough."

Miranda stuck out her tongue. Because they might be virtual strangers, but they were still sisters.

"Astrid called to congratulate her as well," Marley said.

"Wow, that's amazing. How's she doing up there?" Becky kept vague track of Astrid's whereabouts through the NASA web site, but she didn't know much more than that.

"I don't know; she called to congratulate me."

"Well, did she look OK?"

Miranda shrugged. "She looked like she was floating. I wonder if I should try to go to space."

"Why not?" her mother said. "For the Schrader girls, the sky's not the limit."

"Most of the Schrader girls," her father corrected.

At least they had the decency not to throw a surreptitious glance her way.

Oh, wait, no. There it was.

"So how's the library world treating you?"

"Fine, thanks, Marley. It's boring, though. We don't have to talk about it."

"Yes, please," Miranda said. "How do you know what to get in a place like this?"

"Why don't I order for all of us? Is that OK? Becky?"

"Sure," she told Marley. She might have taken a little pride in the fact that her family of geniuses couldn't figure out a restaurant menu, but that would have been petty. And she wasn't here to be petty. She was here to congratulate her sister on her achievement. Even though Miranda didn't think it was a big deal.

"Excuse me a minute." She got up from the table and headed to the ladies' room.

"Where's she going?" her father asked.

"They have bathrooms in restaurants?"

Becky wished she was joining Astrid in space.

It wasn't that Franny Collins wasn't interesting. It was just . . . he couldn't relate.

So far he'd learned that she and her ex split custody of the kids, that he had them on alternate weekends as long as he promised his new girlfriend wouldn't be around, and that this was her first weekend away from them and she was ready to party it up.

That should have been his first sign that this was a bad idea. He didn't feel like partying it up. He was tired. He'd had a long day. And even though he'd called her because he needed a break from Starr's sad eyes and his sister's schooling him on the best way to treat a dog—he didn't love that his sister knew more about this than he did—he kind of wished he was back at home. Sure, Madison had turned on one of those *Housewives* shows, which had effectively propelled him off the couch and into Razor's bar. But listening to Franny talk about her divorce and her kids and her need to party was filling him with a mixture of dread and regret. Dread because he didn't need to party and regret because he sensed Franny was expecting something from him that he wasn't going to give her.

He gave a half-hearted stretch and yawn. "Gosh, I had an early morning. I'm going to have to call it a night after this drink."

"But we've only had one. I'm supposed to be partying!"

Please don't cry please don't cry please don't cry.

"How about one more?"

"You always were such a softy," she told him. He thought about the so-called dog in his apartment and his sister sleeping in the second bedroom.

Yup, he was a softy.

He signaled to the bartender for another round, then excused himself. What he really needed was some air, but he didn't want Franny to see him go outside and think he was going to bolt. So he did what countless dates had done to him over the years: he went to the bathroom.

As he tried to decipher which of the symbols on the doors meant the one he was supposed to use,

the door he was standing in front of opened, right
into his nose.

"Shit! I'm sorry!"

He knew that voice, he thought, as he winced in
pain.

Of course he did.

It was Becky.

"What are you doing here?" she asked him for the
second time that day.

"Don't worry, I'm fine," he said, rubbing his
nose.

"Sorry. Are you OK?"

"Yes. I'm fine. And I'm here with . . . ah, with a
friend."

"What about Starr?"

"Starr is adjusting very well. She's back at my
place, watching reality TV with Madison."

"Oh. Good. That was really nice of you, to step up
and foster her like that."

"That's my name. Heh."

"Heh."

"So." He stepped out of the way as another patron
entered the women's room. "What are you doing
here?"

"Um, just going to the bathroom."

He looked her up and down, taking in her slinky
wrap dress and heels. "You got all dressed up to go
to the bathroom?"

"No. I'm having dinner with my family."

"Oh. I thought . . . you guys made up?"

"We weren't exactly fighting. We're just not close."

"But you're out to dinner?"

"We're celebrating."

"No offense, but you don't look like you're celebrating." She looked pale and very tired. She'd worked even harder than he had today.

He tucked an errant strand of hair behind her ear. Then he put his hand in his pocket because they didn't like each other like that.

She was bumped in the back by the opening ladies'-room door. She took a step toward him and put her hand out, balancing herself against his chest. He was very glad his hand was in his pocket because otherwise he would have covered her hand with his, and they didn't touch each other like that.

"I should get back to my family. We haven't ordered yet."

"Wow, escaping before you've even ordered? Your family must be worse than mine."

"It's not a competition."

"No, you're right. I'm sorry."

"Besides, if it was a competition, I would totally win."

"So . . . congratulations?"

She curtsied. The men's room door opened into his back.

"You should go back to your date."

"She's just a friend."

"That's fine."

"We're going to wrap it up." He hoped. "I've gotta get home and see how Starr's doing. Make sure she's not chewing on Brock's furniture."

"She doesn't have teeth."

"True."

She narrowed her eyes at him. "Are sure you're not falling in love with Starr?"

"I'll admit no such thing. It's just temporary."

"Mm-hmm."

The doors to the men's and the women's rooms opened at the same time. What kind of food did they serve here that the bathrooms were so busy?

"OK, we're clearly in the way. I'll see you around, probably," she said and stuck out her hand.

He took it and shook it.

"Nice to see you again," she said.

"Good luck with the family."

"Shyeah."

"Do you want me to send a bottle of wine over?"

"A bottle of tequila would be better."

"You want to ditch them?" He could just see it. Becky and Foster, hand in hand, dodging bathroom doors and waiters, jumping into his car, driving off into the sunset . . .

"I better not. We don't get together very often."

So much for that. "Well, I'll have a drink in honor of your brave service."

She rolled her eyes and walked away from him. But at least she was smiling.

He watched her sit down at a table of poorly dressed people who didn't even acknowledge her when she returned. The younger guy was deep in conversation with the younger woman at the table: Becky's sister, probably. That left the older couple in matching tweed jackets to be her parents.

She didn't look like her parents. Well, he couldn't really see from afar, but those two looked like their cheek muscles had never experienced a smile, which was decidedly not how Becky looked. She smiled a lot.

Except for right now. She definitely wasn't smiling now, and her shoulders were slumped down toward the bread basket.

Man, she looked glum.

He had a sudden, overwhelming urge to cheer her up.

But he had a date. A date he was trying very hard to end, but his mother would throw a fit if he abandoned Franny at the bar.

By the time he made his way back to Franny, his drink was gone and there was another woman in his seat.

"Foster! Are you OK?" Franny asked.

"Yes," he said, confused.

"You were gone a while."

"Oh. Oh! No, I, uh, ran into a friend."

"Sure you did."

"No, I—" *You know what*, he thought, *I'm not going to argue about this because it's only going to make me look weird.*

Wow, look at him, all giving up on being right.

"You remember Cassie, don't you?" Franny indicated the woman in his former seat.

"Sure," he said, shaking Cassie's hand. He had no idea who she was.

Cassie—whoever she was—laughed. "He has no idea."

"Sure I do! You're—" So much for giving up on being right.

"Cassie Everclear. Our moms are on the Beautify Denver Committee? We made out behind a plant at the Beautify Ball?"

He should definitely remember that. But looking at her, he had no idea.

"Have mercy on him, Cass. That was over twenty years ago."

"Twenty years ago! I wasn't even born then," Cassie said, and she and Franny burst out laughing.

"Wait . . . I remember. You were wearing a big floofy pink dress . . ."

"Yes! And it stuck out from behind the plant and we totally got caught."

"And your brother threatened to beat him up in the parking lot," Franny joyfully reminisced.

"If I recall, and I think I do, your brother *did* beat me up in the parking lot. He broke my nose."

"Poor Foster."

"The wound gives me rakish charm."

"Really? It doesn't look like it was broken."

"My mother may have insisted I get it fixed. But I like to think the memory of it radiates rakish charm. So, Cassie, what are you up to?"

"Who cares about that? I was just getting all the dirt on Franny here. God, can you believe the nerve of her ex?"

He and Franny actually hadn't talked about what

led to her husband becoming an ex. "No, I can't believe it."

"And she tells me you're going to abandon her after one drink?"

"I ordered a second round."

"Sorry, I drank it," Franny explained. "Well, you took forever in the bathroom!"

"I didn't—never mind. And, yes, sad to say, I am about to take Franny home. I just adopted a dog and my sister is there—"

Whatever sympathy he hoped to elicit by bringing up an adopted dog and being a good big brother was totally ignored by Cassie's righteous-sisterhood indignation.

"Well, you can't. I'm taking Franny dancing."

"Do you mind?" Franny asked.

"No! No, that's great. You wanted to go dancing."

"I'll tell my mother you were a good date."

"Wasn't I a good date?"

"Well, you barely listened to me and you kept mooning over those poor dogs you spent all afternoon with at the shelter and how much went into taking a compelling dog photo."

"I did?"

"You did."

"Sorry about that."

"That's OK. Cassie is saving the day, so I'm feeling generous. I'll make sure it gets back to your mom that we had a good time, but not *too* good a time."

Which would mean that his mom would stop pressuring him to call her again.

"You're too good for that rotten ex-husband."

"Thank you!" Cassie shouted. "That's what I was saying!"

He paid the tab and walked them out to Cassie's car. "Don't go too crazy, ladies."

"Don't count on it!"

When they had pulled away, he wandered toward the back of the restaurant, just to make sure he didn't have to go to the bathroom again before the two-minute drive home.

Ah, who was he kidding? He stopped a passing waitress and gave her his card, then headed into the restaurant.

"Persea Americana."

Becky watched her mother tap her chin with her fork, which she recognized as the universal sign for *Mom is tossing something around in her brain, so don't interrupt her.*

"I don't know. It's not quite taxonomically correct, is it?"

Becky sighed. She wasn't sure how long a normal family debated the correct Latin name for the avocado foam that came with their deconstructed nacho appetizer, but she was pretty sure it wasn't from the arrival of said appetizer through the clearing of their dinner plates. Two courses. Two courses of arguments for and against mere Latin translation as an adequate taxonomical designation.

If the food wasn't so good, she would have left long ago.

"You're wasting your time on hypotheticals," her father said, not for the first time.

"Yes, because there's no place for hypotheticals in *science*," her mother hissed. "It's comments like that that remind me how this one"—she stuck her thumb out at Becky—"went into *library* science."

"Library science *is* a science," Becky said, because she knew it made her family furious and they were going to blame her for ruining a perfectly good evening anyway, so why not?

But before anyone could get any heat behind their arguments, dessert arrived. Just in time, too. She could take a lot more of what her family dished out if it always came with chocolate lava cake.

And . . . a bottle of wine.

Had they ordered wine?

"I hope you don't mind," said a voice behind her, and Becky had a sudden urge to crawl under the table. It was one thing for her family to tear her down in public; it was another thing entirely for them to do it in front of Foster.

She looked up at him. He was smiling. At her parents.

"What are you doing?" she hissed.

He winked at her. "I'm great with parents."

The nerve of that condescending . . . if she wasn't so annoyed, she'd be thrilled watching him learn how not-great her parents were.

"Hello?" her father said. "What?"

"Hi," Foster said, reaching across the table to shake his hand. "Foster Deacon. I work with your daughter at Polak and Glassmeyer."

"You don't work at Polak and Glassmeyer," her mother said to Miranda.

Becky closed her eyes. Took a deep breath. Opened them.

"No." Foster laughed, although it sounded a bit forced. "With Becky."

"Rebecca? You work at Polak and Glassmeyer?"

"Yes, Mom."

"What's Polak and Glassmeyer?"

"What's this?" Her father picked the bottle of wine out of the ice bucket, dripping water all over his meringue.

"I saw Becky sitting here and I remembered she said you were celebrating, so I thought . . ."

Nobody said anything.

"So . . . congratulations." He nodded at Miranda. Miranda blinked at him.

"Thank you, Foster," Becky said, hoping that if she feigned politeness, he would just go away. "That was very nice. Wasn't that very nice, Miranda?"

"Yes, thanks. Hi, I'm Marley." Marley stood up and shook Foster's hand. "Miranda's partner."

"Ah," Foster said, and then Becky remembered that he didn't know her sister's name or who her parents were or any of that stuff, and she should probably be polite and ask him to join them, but she just couldn't seem to get the words out of her mouth.

"Would you like to join us?" Marley asked, and Becky cursed him and his good manners.

She also cursed the waiter, who just then appeared with an extra chair.

"Don't you have to go back to your date?" she whispered as Foster settled in next to her.

"She's not a date, she's just a friend," he said, opening the wine and filling everyone's glasses. "She went off with someone more fun."

"Gosh, I can't imagine anyone more fun than you."

"I saw you were still here and I thought you might need rescuing."

"I don't need rescuing."

"So what do you do at . . . sorry, what was it?" Marley asked.

"Polak and Glassmeyer. I'm an attorney."

"Are *you* an attorney?" her mother asked.

"No, she's a librarian," Miranda reminded her.

"Oh, right. Library *science*."

"How about a toast?" Foster offered, raising his glass.

"To what?" her father asked.

"To Miranda," Marley said, raising his glass as well. The others followed suit. "I'm so happy you're getting the recognition you deserve."

"Finally," Miranda muttered, but she melted into Marley's side hug, which was just about the only affectionate thing Becky had ever seen her do.

She drank down her whole glass, fast.

Everyone drank their wine—much more sensibly— and murmured how good it was, and Becky could see Foster's head blowing up to match the size of his ego. He was good with families. Ha.

"So, Miranda, Becky didn't get a chance to tell me what you're being honored for."

Miranda raised an eyebrow at him. "A MacArthur Fellowship."

"I know that, I mean . . ."

"You mean what for?" Miranda pursed her lips in concentration. "I'm not sure if I can explain it in simple enough terms for you."

Foster choked on his wine. Becky slapped him on the back.

"No offense," Miranda said when Marley elbowed her gently in the side. "What? It's complicated. You try to explain it."

Marley opened his mouth, but Foster cut him off. "No, that's fine. It's enough just to celebrate. Unless . . . you're not, like, making bombs or clubbing seals, right?" He laughed at his joke but stopped. Probably because no one else was laughing.

"I see you have about as much of an understanding of the sciences as Becky does," her father said.

Foster looked at her, confused. She shook her head to try to get him to drop it. She should have known Foster wouldn't give up on a rescue mission.

"I'm sorry, why do you keep saying Becky doesn't understand science?"

"She's a *librarian*," her mother said, as if that explained everything.

Foster looked to Marley for help. Marley shook his head, too.

"They don't think library science is a real science, therefore they think nothing in my life has meaning or worth, and remember when I told you my family and I aren't close? This is why. Excuse me."

She got up from the table and grabbed her coat and purse. She didn't look to see if Foster followed.

He finally caught up with her as she was unlocking her car, which was parked at one of the meters.

"Hey!" he shouted, and she whirled on him so fast he ducked.

"Foster!" She held her hand over her chest. "Jesus. Do not sneak up on women alone at night."

"Sorry. Sorry, I didn't think . . . are you OK?"

"Hold on, let me just get my heart out of my throat."

"I mean about back there." He pointed vaguely in the direction of the restaurant.

"Oh that. Yeah. When I reach my limit with my family, that's kind of it."

"I can see why."

"Well, I would have made it through the whole meal if you hadn't interfered."

"I was trying to help."

"Even though I told you I was fine?"

"You didn't look fine, that's why—"

She stopped him with a hand over his mouth. "I know you meant well," she said, "but I also don't care, because you did exactly what I asked you not to do and I already have enough trouble dealing with my family and it would have been great if you had just let me do it on my own."

"Parents normally love me."

She rolled her eyes. "Foster. I'm going home. I'm going to take a hot bath and drink a bottle of wine and pretend this evening never happened."

"Do you want . . ."

"I want to do just what I described, and I don't want you involved. I don't need you, Foster. I just need to go home."

"Fine," he said, but she'd already climbed in the car and driven away.

He drove himself home and let himself in as quietly as he could, expecting to see Starr and Madison still zoned out on the couch, half-hoping they would both wake up and be excited to see him. But the apartment was dark and quiet, which he chose to assume meant all was well. He snuck past the second bedroom and saw Madison sound asleep, but there was no sign of Starr anywhere. He slipped off his shoes and made a quick tour of the apartment, but he couldn't find her. The door had been closed, and the windows, too, so she had to be in here somewhere.

He checked her crate and behind the couch. All he wanted to do was crawl into bed and nurse his wounded pride, and he was about to do just that and let Starr figure out her first night however she wanted to, when he heard a small squeak from under his bed. He got down on his knees. There she was, pressed up against the wall. He stuck his hand out toward her, but she just watched him from her safe distance.

"Don't you care that I need love, too?" he asked, grateful that nobody else was awake to hear him. Starr continued to watch him but didn't move.

Well, she seemed comfortable enough, so he got

up and brushed his teeth and put on some flannel pants. She was still under there when he was done, so he just climbed into bed, alone. Which was good, because he didn't really want her sleeping in his bed, if for no other reason than she was badly in need of a bath. He got into bed and was just drifting off to sleep thinking about how sad Becky looked at her family celebration, when he heard a shuffling scratch on the edge of his comforter. He leaned over his bed and there was Starr, tongue hanging out and butt wiggling.

"No," he said quietly. "You're not sleeping in bed with me."

She stuck out her paw and scratched the comforter again.

"Remember those throw pillows on the couch? Those were comfortable. Why don't you sleep on one of those?"

She turned and walked away. He lay back down, congratulating himself on choosing to (temporarily) adopt such a smart dog.

Then he heard toenails on the hardwood floor and, a second later, a weight landed on his leg with a soft thump.

"What the—"

But he didn't have a chance. Starr was climbing up toward the pillows. She sniffed his hair and licked his cheek—she really did smell—then pawed at the comforter again.

"You smell," he told her.

She pawed at the edge of the comforter.

He sighed. "Fine. Just for tonight." He lifted the edge of the sheet and Starr crawled inside, curling herself into a soft, stinky ball next to his hip.

It was fine.

It was just temporary.

At least somebody needed him.

Chapter Ten

Becky stood on the porch of Dakota's duplex, hoping the box of bakery goods would make up for the fact that she'd shown up uninvited. But she needed her best friend. It was as close to a drama emergency as Becky was ever going to get in a life she had worked hard to keep normal and drama-free.

Besides, she and Dakota had known each other forever. Dakota knew Becky needed to be scraped off the ground whenever her family was involved.

She decided she wasn't going to mention Foster's involvement. Dakota would accuse her of falling in love—which she wasn't; that was ridiculous—but then Dakota would accuse her of protesting too much, and Becky just couldn't deal with that kind of mental exercise right now. She just needed a friend.

And some carbs.

She juggled her shopping bag—because if baked goods didn't earn her friend's forgiveness, she knew mimosas would—and rang the doorbell again.

She heard footsteps and figured she must have woken Dakota up because she didn't usually sound like a herd of cattle clomping down the stairs. But the door didn't open.

Becky was about to ring again—what was going on in there?—when the door opened. And there was Dakota, one hand on the door.

She didn't see Becky, but how could she? She had her tongue down Bullhorn's throat.

"Oh!" Becky dropped the baked goods.

Dakota whipped around.

And slammed the door in her face.

A second later, the door opened again and Dakota was there with an apologetic smile.

"I don't suppose you didn't see that?" she asked.

"See what?" Becky answered, because she was a good friend.

Dakota sighed. "Never mind. Come in."

Dakota reached for the shopping bag and Becky leaned down to pick up the bakery box, which thankfully had survived the fall unopened. A little dented, but mostly unharmed.

Sort of like Becky.

"Here, let me get that." And then Bullhorn was down on her level, taking the box from her hand and holding the door open for her.

She followed him inside and up the stairs to Dakota's apartment. Dakota was already in the kitchen, unpacking the OJ and reaching for her vintage champagne glasses.

"Hi," she said brightly. "Hi."

"Hi," Becky said, and she couldn't help but smile

as Bullhorn kicked at the carpet like a kid about to receive a punishment.

"Nice to see you again, Bullhorn."

"Hi, Becky."

"Sorry I missed you yesterday at the shelter."

"Yup."

"So," Dakota said, clapping her hands together. "Who wants a drink?"

A mimosa and a half later, Becky finally got the truth out of Dakota.

"Fine, yes, we've been seeing each other."

"How many times?"

Dakota started counting softly under her breath. She looked up at the ceiling as if the answer to how many times she'd gone out with a guy named Bullhorn was written in the stucco.

"I don't know exactly. Maybe twenty?"

"Twenty? It's only been a week! What'd you do, go on three dates in one day?"

"Oh! You're talking about dates! Yeah, we haven't really been on any dates."

"Then what are you talking about? Twenty what? Oh." The mimosas were making her slow. Plus, she was having a hard time picturing Bullhorn in any kind of sexual situation. Fortunately, he had left just as soon as Becky got there.

"Don't let that frat-boy exterior fool you. Bullhorn has hidden depths."

"And yet he still goes by the name Bullhorn."

"He was a cheerleader in college."

"Wow. I never thought you'd go for a cheerleader."

"Hey, he's pretty limber. And he owns a brewery."

"A cheerleading brewery?"

"No. Ha ha. It's the one on South Broadway, the one that's always on the *Westword Best of Denver* list."

"He owns that brewery? But that place is, like, cool."

"Yeah."

"And breweries are a lot of work."

"I know. And here's something else: he reads."

"Books?"

Dakota nodded. "For fun."

"Wow."

"I told you. Hidden depths."

"So . . . are you getting serious?"

"Serious? Beck, it's only been a week. People don't just, like, shack up permanently in a week."

"I know."

"Do you? I seem to recall you picking out china patterns before you even sleep with a guy."

"I do *not* pick out china patterns." She was much more interested in casual dinnerware. "Anyway, I've turned over a new leaf."

"Really? So if a guy in a bad suit walked through this door, you wouldn't jump all over him?"

"No."

"Not even if he wanted to give you a tour of his house with the white picket fence?"

"The white picket fence is just a metaphor. But I told you, I'm done. Reset."

"But that was back when he was just an anonymous lumberjack. Now he's Foster."

"Yeah, Foster who's an attorney, and I'm done with lawyers."

"Foster who adopted a sad old dog."

"He's just fostering her. I would have done it if I could've gotten out of that part of my lease."

"Hmm. If only you knew some lawyer who could help you with that."

"Besides, Foster is a genius, so even if I hadn't sworn off lawyers—which I have—I will never swear on geniuses."

"Swear on?"

"That's the opposite of swear off, right?"

"Not sure about that. Maybe we should ask a genius."

"He's not that kind of genius. He's a legal genius. One of the greatest legal minds of our generation."

"Did he tell you that?"

"No, AALL did."

"Should that mean something to me?"

"The American Association of Law Libraries. And the American Bar Association and the Columbia Law Review and just about every publication that writes anything about intellectual property."

"So, things normal people don't care about."

"I care and I'm normal."

"You sure about that?"

"Trust me."

"I'm just saying, it might be okay to bend your no-lawyers rule."

"Bend it? I just started following it! Because you told me to!"

"Maybe I was wrong."

"No. You're never wrong."

"Say that one more time, for posterity."

"About love, at least."

"I am apparently dating a guy named Bullhorn."

"Besides, Foster is a jerk."

"No, he's not."

"Fine. But he's condescending at work."

"So don't date him at work."

"This is so unfair. You told me no feelings, so I did it. No feelings! And so even though he's really great and it was the best sex of my life, I'm not having feelings for him, okay? I'm not."

"OK, OK." Dakota got up to refill their drinks. Because Becky definitely needed more alcohol.

"So . . . how was dinner last night?"

She took the bottle of champagne from Dakota. If she was going to get into this, she definitely needed more alcohol.

"That good, huh?"

Becky shrugged. "It was fine. It was the longest we've sat together at a table in . . . I think my entire life."

"Your family. I don't know how you came from them."

"Neither do they."

"Not all geniuses are like your parents, you know."

She'd known Dakota since middle school, when she was the weird new kid who talked funny. Becky felt bad for her—and was sort of fascinated by her Southern accent—and her pity turned into an unbreakable friendship. Which meant they knew everything about each other. Which meant Dakota had been to her parents' house and seen the complete lack of comfortable social furniture and the absence of any of that trivial conversation that makes a family feel connected. She'd heard her parents tease her about her C report card and her choice to go to a state school and how library science wasn't a real science. Dakota didn't live with it, but she'd seen a little of what it was like to grow up around geniuses.

So despite all the evidence that Foster was a normal, nice guy, she had to be on guard. She wasn't going to throw her heart out to another genius and have it thrown back in her face because it wasn't good enough.

Foster stared at the corner of the couch where a naked mole-rat sat staring back at him.

That wasn't nice. So Starr wasn't the fluffball he'd expected when he'd picked her up from a six-hour appointment at the groomer. She did look better without all those painful-looking mats covering her. And once they got back home, her shell-shocked look subsided and she seemed a lot happier. Apparently, she didn't have a wonky ear; it just needed to be freed from the mess of hair.

Poor girl, he thought as he reached out to scratch her naked little back. She was going to be cold. Good thing he'd bought her a sweater when he went to the pet store to get more food.

A sweater, a puffy vest, a fleece, a dog bed, and a whole bag of toys that turned out to be too big for her. But they were fluffy and she liked to cuddle with them.

"What are you doing to me?" he asked her now. "I used to be a man with dignity." Now he had a chupacabra who cuddled.

A chupacabra with a wardrobe.

Starr still couldn't be convinced to put on any of the sweaters, and Foster decided she'd had such a traumatic day that he wouldn't force her. She'd be cold when they went outside for a walk, but that wouldn't be for a while. Instead, he just turned up the heat and took off his sweater.

They'd just chill out together, get to know each other a little better.

For Starr, this meant staring at him from the other end of the couch.

"I'm a genius, you know."

Starr just looked back at him.

Foster sighed. What was he supposed to do with a dog?

"Do you want to play fetch or something?" When she didn't respond, he picked up one of the squeaky toys he'd bought. This one was in the shape of a football. He squeezed it, then let it sail down the corridor.

Starr perked up enough to watch it go, then turned her attention back to Foster.

"Fetch," he said hopefully. "I don't suppose you'll be one of those dogs I can train to bring me a beer, are you?"

Starr rested her head on her legs, but didn't take her eyes off Foster.

Poor pathetic little beast, he thought. He wanted to scoop her up and squeeze her and scratch behind her ears. But he'd already tried that and all he'd gotten was a retreat to the other end of the couch and this stare down.

"Do you want to watch TV?" he asked. "Why am I even asking you? I'm the alpha dog here. We're just going to do what I want to do. Which, fortunately, is not playing fetch. That was just a test."

He picked up the remote and flicked on the television. Starr didn't move, but she didn't seem upset by the noise either.

"TV it is," he said with finality, because he was the alpha of the house. He put his feet up on the coffee table and flipped through the channels until he found a movie with lots of explosions.

Every so often he'd sneak a look over at Starr, just to make sure she was still there. She was, and she eventually closed her eyes and started snoring.

God, even her snore was cute.

This was all Becky's fault. She was the one who'd convinced him to adopt Starr. Foster her. Whatever. If Becky hadn't been giving him that look of adoration, he never would have been coerced.

That wasn't fair. Becky was more . . . coercion adjacent. Madison was the one who'd really done him in. And now where was she? She'd turned on the waterworks, sent him home with a mop dog, then had the nerve to have an appointment with her math tutor.

Maybe he could call Becky. Maybe he could convince her Starr was her fault, and then she'd come over and they could stare at her cute little hairless face together.

No. That was ridiculous. Of course he wasn't going to do that. He was just going to sit at home and watch this explosion-heavy movie and let his temporary dog get acclimated to his sublet apartment.

Foster put his feet up on the couch and stretched out. Starr immediately moved from her perch on the pillow and climbed across his body.

"I thought you were asleep," he accused her, but she just stared back at him like he was missing the most obvious point in the world. Then she squished herself between his body and the couch and rested her head on his ribs. She closed her eyes. So did Foster. And in a minute, they were both snoring.

Chapter Eleven

It had been a pretty good week. Nobody sent her any last-minute urgent research requests, three of her dogs got adopted, and Foster sent her a picture of Starr and said he hoped she'd recovered from the dinner-that-shall-not-be-named. She probably owed him an apology, but because they were more or less normal and professional around each other, she just kept her head down. She didn't need to see him any more than was absolutely necessary. Not because she was falling for him, but because every time she talked to him, he seemed to do something that annoyed her. Like show up and try to charm her parents into being nice to her.

The nerve.

Then, over the weekend, she hadn't run into him at the shelter, which wasn't disappointing at all. It was a relief. The week before, she'd seemed to run into him everywhere she went, so this was a nice change of pace.

Because she didn't care about seeing him.

Also, because no Foster at the shelter meant he hadn't had some kind of breakdown and returned Starr. In fact, Maddie said Foster was embarrassingly in love with the dog, even though he denied it. He'd bought her sweaters. Plural.

So when she happened to be on his floor to deliver some misdirected mail, she just poked her head in to ask how Starr was doing. That was it. God, like there was another reason she would talk to him?

He was staring at his computer. He wasn't exactly pulling his hair out, but he was definitely using lots of force to push it out of its normal, neat position.

She shouldn't bother him.

But then he looked up at the doorway.

And smiled at her.

Well, it would be rude to walk away now.

"Hi," she said. "I was just . . . passing through." Like a stalker. To be fair, she was stalking the dog.

"Come on in. Sit down." He stood up and walked around the desk and pulled out a chair for her. His hair was still sticking up. Without thinking, she reached up and brushed it down.

"Oh! Sorry. You're, uh . . . it's better now."

He frantically flattened out the rest of his hair. "I was concentrating. Sometimes I . . . you know."

Why were they acting like two kids who'd never spoken to someone of the opposite sex before?

"So . . . how've you been?" he asked.

"Fine, good."

"Convincing."

"No, I'm fine. And . . . Sorry about last weekend. After the dinner with my family, I mean."

"There's nothing to apologize for."

"Okay, thanks. I appreciate that."

"Unless you want to reconsider your opinion that I'm not good with parents. For the record, I am."

"Despite all evidence to the contrary?"

"Hey, you're the one who insists your parents aren't normal."

"Don't make me laugh," she said, but too late. She was laughing.

He didn't say anything for a minute, just watched her. She was starting to worry that there was something on her face when he said, "Your family is terrible."

"Tell me about it."

"They don't deserve you."

And now she was sure there was something on her face because it felt all hot and weird.

She cleared her throat. "So that's why I want a normal life. Because for me, that's not normal."

"No kidding."

"Anyway, I didn't come here to talk about my family. I came here to talk about your dog."

"Oh! She got a haircut!" He took out his phone and started scrolling through the dozens of pictures he'd taken of . . . well, she assumed it was Starr. Starr looked a little . . . naked. Except for in the pictures where she was wearing a sweater.

"You're really smitten with that dog, aren't you?"

"What? No. She just needed to be taken care of, that's all. It was a favor to Madison. And to you."

"Really?"

"Really. So you owe me one."

"Oh really. And what do I owe you?"

He tapped his finger against his chin and made a maniacal face. Still cute, though. "I'm going to hold on to that marker for a bit."

There it was again. That thing on her face making her feel all hot.

"Well, um. I should let you get back to work."

"Sure. Thanks for stopping by."

"Thanks for showing me pictures of your dog."

"Foster dog."

"Foster's dog."

"Ha ha."

She turned and was almost out the door when he called after her: "Normal's overrated."

Ha. What did he know? He wasn't normal at all.

The first thing Foster wondered was whether he could bring Starr to the office because he was going to be working such late hours. But Claire—who was an intern, not a clerk—was allergic to everything, so that probably wouldn't work.

The second thing he thought was that he had a long way to go to get this team up to speed if they were going to start giving evidence later that month.

The third thing was whether he could get a specific librarian assigned to their case.

Better focus on thing two. Especially because they had just finished a conference call with Goliath.

Goliath was based right outside of Denver. He didn't know why his folks couldn't go across town to meet with them, or the team couldn't come here and meet in one of P&G's conference rooms, but that was the way they wanted it and they were the client. The junior associates had a pool going about the reason they wouldn't meet in person. So far his favorite was that Goliath was just a cover for a super-hero conglomerate and their identities couldn't be compromised. His least favorite was that they were nudists.

Whatever it was, they weren't messing around. Which was good; he didn't waste his time on clients who messed around. But that also meant his team had to stop thinking about superheroes and start thinking about document review.

Boxes and boxes of document review.

"OK, let's divide this up." He pointed at the junior associate who thought the people at Goliath were nudists. "We've got a long night ahead of us. Order us some food." He flipped through what he thought was the newest box. "Claire, is this stuff we just got from the library?"

Claire looked a little nervous. "About that . . ."

To: Rebecca Schrader
From: Foster Deacon
Subject: Articles

Hi Becky,

I just spoke to Claire and she said you had trouble getting the issues of National Geographic *we need. Can you help me out?*

Foster

To: Foster Deacon
From: Rebecca Schrader
Subject: Re: Articles

Foster—

As I explained to Claire, we don't subscribe to National Geographic, *nor do we subscribe to* Modern Homesteader. *I sent on all the articles we have access to.*

Becky

To: Rebecca Schrader
From: Foster Deacon
Subject: Re: Re: Articles

Can we get a subscription?

To: Foster Deacon
From: Rebecca Schrader
Subject: Re: Re: Re: Articles

Are we doing this again? I can get electronic access to back issues of NG, *which I gave to Claire.*

R

To: Rebecca Schrader
From: Foster Deacon
Subject: Re: Re: Re: Re: Articles

What about Modern Homesteader?

F

To: Foster Deacon
From: Rebecca Schrader
Subject: Re: Re: Re: Re: Re: Articles

Modern Homesteader *isn't available online.*

To: Rebecca Schrader
From: Foster Deacon
Subject: Re: Re: Re: Re: Re: Re: Articles

I know. I couldn't find their web site. See? I did try. But I need what they've got on home apiaries.

It's not in one of those fancy databases you love so much?

To: Foster Deacon
From: Rebecca Schrader
Subject: Re: Re: Re: Re: Re: Re: Re: Articles

*OH THE DATABASES WHY DIDN'T I THINK TO
LOOK IT UP IN A DATABASE.*

Modern Homesteader *is published by a
polygamist cult in the Utah desert who think the
internet is a tool of the devil. So, no, back issues
aren't indexed in a database. I can try to track
down which random office supply store they
make their copies at if the client will spring for
a road trip.*

*Also, how the hell is any information from a cult
that doesn't let women wear pants going to help
you with the case?*

B

To: Rebecca Schrader
From: Foster Deacon
Subject: Re: Re: Re: Re: Re: Re: Re: Re: Articles

*You know I can't talk about the specifics of the
case.*

*Also, I didn't know it was a religious
publication.*

F

To: Foster Deacon
From: Rebecca Schrader
Subject: Re: Re: Re: Re: Re: Re: Re: Re: Re: Articles

This brief lesson in information literacy was brought to you by your friendly librarian, who already gave this information to your intern.

I hope you get stung by a bee.

B

To: Rebecca Schrader
From: Foster Deacon
Subject: Re: Re: Re: Re: Re: Re: Re: Re: Re: Re: Articles

Becky—

The species of pollinator in question doesn't sting.

F

To: Foster Deacon
From: Rebecca Schrader
Subject: Re: Re: Re: Re: Re: Re: Re: Re: Re: Re: Re: Articles

You just had to get the last word, didn't you?

To: Rebecca Schrader
From: Foster Deacon
Subject: Re: Re: Re: Re: Re: Re: Re: Re: Re: Re: Re:
Re: Articles

No, I didn't.

To: Rebecca Schrader
From: Foster Deacon
Subject: Re: Re: Re: Re: Re: Re: Re: Re: Re: Re: Re:
Re: Re: Articles

Wait, I see what you did there.

To: Rebecca Schrader
From: Foster Deacon
Subject: Re: Re: Re: Re: Re: Re: Re: Re: Re: Re: Re:
Re: Re: Re: Articles

Hey! No fair!

<<Microsoft Outlook has recalled the last three
messages>>

Just when she was starting to like him.

Becky watched as the P&G email program ate the
last three messages he'd sent. Like she hadn't already
opened them and seen him being a total brat. Ha.

Ha ha ha.

She watched her screen for another minute. Then
another.

Not because she was waiting for him to write

back. No, he'd already done that. And recalled them. So . . . technically, she'd had the last word.

"Mail call."

She jumped out of her seat when Will stuck his head through her office door.

"Whoa, there, what's up, jumpy?"

"Nothing! Nothing. Hi, Will." She held out her hand for the mail and took her eyes off her computer screen.

Foster hoped that email recall worked. God, he was a brat. No, he was just tired. And sick of reading and delegating and being an adult.

He needed to stretch his legs and clear his mind.

"I'll be back in a second," he told his team, then went in search of something to help him focus.

He probably wasn't going to find it in the library, but he ended up there anyway.

"Hi, Foster. Can I help you with something?" Anne, the head librarian, watched as he stood dumbly in front of the reference desk.

He didn't actually have a reference question. And he didn't have a problem with Anne. She just wasn't the librarian he was looking for.

Not that he was really looking for her.

If he was really looking for her, he would have been annoyed to see her rush out of her office, her coat half on, and sneak down the backstairs to the exit.

Good thing he had nothing to say to Becky. Cuz she was gone.

Chapter Twelve

Becky didn't like being in the office so late. She almost never was. Once every other year or so, some crazy emergency request would come through for a gigantic client, but that kind of stuff hardly happened in firms like P&G.

Of course she wasn't working now. No, she was looking for her cell phone. It wasn't in the bottom of her purse, where all her other possessions went to die, and it wasn't anywhere in her car. She knew this because Dakota had driven to her house, pissed that she wasn't responding to her texts, and made Becky look for it there.

She knew she'd had it earlier in the day, so the only other place it could be was at work. But she never left her phone at work.

Of course she didn't usually run out of the office when she heard a lawyer speaking to Anne out at the reference desk. But these were special circumstances. The voice had belonged to Foster, and she'd already wasted too much of her day waiting to see if he'd throw her some kind of flirty bone. She had some pride, dammit.

And she had a phone. Right there on her desk. And there were six messages from Dakota with varying degrees of annoyance at her flaking out on their dinner plans. She sent her a reply now, proving that she wasn't, in fact, ignoring her, and that she'd demonstrated it by showing up at the office at ten at night in her yoga pants and at-home hair. Why hadn't she just remembered that she was all flustered when she left because she'd heard Foster talking to Anne and she hadn't wanted to see him so she'd snuck out as fast as she could?

Why she didn't want to see him, she didn't know. She'd just heard his voice and run.

Leaving her phone behind.

Well, as far as the end of the world went, this probably wasn't going to contribute too much to the apocalypse. Although she did owe Dakota an apology.

Found my phone. You are forgiven.

Is that an apology?

Yes.

You're spending way too much time with lawyers.

Ha ha, she thought, and slipped the phone into her bag. She had to get out of there. She didn't like being at the office with no one else there. Sure there were security guards and cleaners, but when the library was empty like this, with nothing but shelves offering plenty of places for serial killers to hide . . .

She froze at the door to her office. There it was again. A noise. Coming from the stacks.

She should call 911. She should call downstairs for the security guard. She should get the hell out of here because there was clearly a serial killer . . . singing?

She cocked her head, listening. The singing went from mumbled humming to practically shouting the words. She recognized the words—she'd sung that emo hit many times in the car with her friends back in high school. That wasn't the tune she'd sung, on account of it being totally not the way the song was meant to sound. But, well, when you feel it, you feel it.

She was biologically incapable of passing up an opportunity to razz someone on their embarrassing behavior—even if it meant razzing a serial killer—so she walked toward the back of the library, prepared to sneak up on the cleaning guy and high-five him for his attempt to hit those high notes.

But as she got nearer, she saw it wasn't the cleaning guy. It was a guy working at the table squirreled away back there, the one she used when she had to hide from people and get stuff done. The table was covered in papers and there, with his back to her, singing his heart out . . .

It was Foster.

Foster wasn't a good singer.

She fumbled for her phone because she was a jerk and started to take a video. She didn't plan on doing anything with the video, except just maybe look at it sometimes when she felt the world was against her. She could imagine the comfort she would take from watching this legal genius, one of the finest minds in his field, bellowing—there was no other word for it—about anger and heartache.

So much comfort.

God, he was a terrible singer.

And he was really into it. Head tilted back to reach the high notes—which he didn't, bless his heart—eyes squeezed shut against the pain. He was really feeling it. And then he started feeling the drum solo, which had him banging his pencil against the desk. His gusto, though, got him tangled in his earbuds, and one slipped out.

Becky should have taken that moment to slip into the stacks, to sneak out without Foster noticing. She really should have. But as he turned to retrieve his lost headphones, he saw her.

And he froze.

She smiled weakly, holding back her laughter.

"Hi," he said over the tinny refrain of the heartbroken singer. He fumbled for his phone and turned the music off. He cleared his throat and turned back to her. "Uh, I don't suppose you got here just this second?"

"Nope."

"So . . . you saw that?"

"I saw it. And I heard it."

He squeezed his eyes shut. "Yup, of course you did."

"And I recorded it."

"I'll give you twelve million dollars to destroy that recording."

"You're not a very good singer, you know."

"I know. That's why I turn the music up, to drown out the sound of my own terrible voice. What are you doing here anyway?"

She held up her phone. "Left it on my desk. What are you doing here?"

"Document review."

"No, I mean, what are you doing in the library?"

"Couldn't concentrate in my office. It's too quiet."

"Oh." She walked toward the table and leaned against a corner. "And your headphones don't work in your office?"

"They do, but the junior associates are in there."

"More document review?"

"So much document review."

"So you came up to the nice, quiet library so you could sing your heart out in peace."

"It helps me concentrate."

"You looked really focused on that document."

"I am. I was. I was taking a break."

"A song break."

"Yes, and after the song's over, I'll be able to re-focus."

"Ah. So . . . I should let you get back to it."

"Yeah." She didn't move, and he wasn't giving her

any signals that she should move. "So, uh, what have you been up to tonight?"

"I was supposed to meet Dakota for dinner and I was waiting for her to text me."

"But she didn't?"

"Oh, she did. But I didn't get it because my phone was here. And I got all pissy with her because I thought she was blowing me off and it turned into kind of a thing."

"You guys in a fight?"

She snorted. "No. We're not children. I apologized." Sort of. "But it's too late for dinner."

"Is it?" He looked at his watch. "Damn. No wonder I'm hungry. What did those damn juniors do with all the food? Did you eat?"

She shook her head. She shouldn't have dinner with him. She should go home. She'd just come here to get her phone. She had some soup to reheat.

But her perch on the edge of the table had her thighs really close to his hands and that got her all confused. Soup was what her body needed, not his hands.

Soup.

His hand brushed her thigh.

Soup, dammit.

"I think I've done all I can for tonight," he said. He didn't touch her again, but the look in his eyes said that he very much wanted to.

She did a quick mental assessment:

1) He was a genius, and therefore not a good match for her.

2) She was looking for a good match and she had to focus on not wasting her time with bad matches.

3) But even if he wasn't a good match, there was no reason why she couldn't enjoy the parts of him that did match. The parts that weren't his brain. The parts that were muscles. And. Other parts.

4) But if she kept giving in to her physical attraction, she was probably putting herself in danger of making another bad match.

5) But he was a genius and she was in no way in the market for a genius match. She could safely continue their physical-only relationship without the danger of falling in love.

6) But since it was only physical, it should be no big deal to be responsible and take her phone and go home and eat her soup.

That's what decided her, in the end.
Nobody should give up sexual fulfillment for soup.

Becky sat back further on the desk, and it was all Foster could do to keep his hands from following her. Then she spread her legs so they were on either side of his.

If he hadn't spent the last six hours painstakingly nitpicking the piles of paper on the table, he would have brushed them aside and ravished her right there.

"Hold on," he said and stood up to make quick piles of his papers. Then he piled them neatly on the floor under the table, out of harm's way.

"OK," he said, standing up. "Sorry, I don't want you to think I'm not interested, it's just—"

"Oh, I understand that you're interested." She tugged him closer by the waist of his pants. Yeah, that thing probably gave him away.

"So I'm not giving out mixed signals?" he asked, planting his hands on either side of her hips.

"Nope," she said, shaking her head so her lips rubbed gently across his.

"Good," he whispered, and then it was on.

He crushed his mouth to hers and felt her arms go tight around his shoulders. He circled her waist with his arms and pulled her close to him, close enough to feel the evidence. She gasped and he said a prayer of thanks to the gods of thin yoga pants.

They kissed and necked and grabbed and squeezed until they were both panting. His shirt was half undone and hers halfway over her head. Jesus, he needed her.

"Do you have a—" she asked, but she got cut off because he put his hand down those yoga pants. She swore into his neck. "Please tell me you have a condom."

He stopped moving.

She wiggled a little, then whimpered. "No condom?"

He shook his head.

"Not even, like, tucked away in a secret stash in your office?"

He rested his forehead against hers. "What kind of perv do you think I am?"

She kissed him. "A terrible one."

"Terrible?" He kissed her back.

"A good perv would have a condom."

He felt her smile against his lips and he took her head between his hands so he could kiss her deeper because he loved that sassy mouth.

"We should stop," she whispered.

He sucked on her neck.

"Foster."

He squeezed her breasts.

"Foster, please."

He kissed a trail down her chest, down her stomach, down, down, taking her yoga pants and her panties with him.

"Foster, what are you doing?" She was totally breathless, but she figured it out soon enough. And as he tossed her legs over his shoulders, he heard her muffled gasps and showed her that he was a damn good perv.

Chapter Thirteen

"He did what?"

Becky looked around to make sure nobody'd heard. But of course they'd heard. Dakota was shouting.

"Shh. You heard me," she whispered.

"I think I heard you. Did you say that he went—"

Becky slapped a hand over her best friend's mouth. "Yes."

"In the library?" Dakota whispered.

"Yes." Becky thought her head might have caught on fire. But, no. She was just blushing.

"Holy shit." Dakota fanned herself. "I think I love this guy."

Ha, love. Now they were on safe ground. "Well, I don't, so don't you worry about me."

Dakota gave her a puzzled look. "Are you sure?"

"That I don't love him? Absolutely."

"No, that I shouldn't worry about you. I mean, are you unwell? What year is this?"

"Shut up. What do you mean?"

"I mean, here's a guy who moved back to town to take care of his younger sister, who rescues decrepit dogs—"

"Starr is not decrepit!"

"She was. And who, in the absence of an appropriate prophylactic solution, goes down on you on a library table."

"Stop making it sound like a big deal!"

Dakota raised her eyebrow. "It wasn't a big deal? How many times did you come?"

"Dakota!"

"Well?"

Becky stuck her head into the menu. "Three," she whispered.

"Three!" And Dakota was shouting again. "You know, I think I hate you."

"What's up your butt?"

Foster was really starting to reconsider this whole spending-quality-time-with-his-sister thing. For starters, she was always showing up unannounced. (Not totally unannounced. Whenever she left the house, his mother called to tell him she was on her way and to text her when she got there so she knew Madison wasn't sneaking off with her inappropriate—his mother's word—friends.) But then Maddie had to cap it off by being way too perceptive for a teenager.

"There's nothing up my butt, squirt." Because he definitely wasn't going to tell his sixteen-year-old sister about his uncontrollable physical attraction to Becky. Especially not in the middle of a hiking trail.

Well, anywhere, really. But definitely not on a trail.

"You look like Dad."

Starr stopped to smell more grass. He wondered if this grass smelled any different from the fourteen other patches of grass she'd stopped to sniff.

"Wait a minute, what do you mean I look like Dad?"

"He's always got that pissy work face."

"Pissy work face?"

"That's it. You're doing it now. It's the face he makes whenever he's home but wishes he was back at the office doing . . . I don't know, doing lawyer things."

Foster tried very hard not to think about the last time he was at the office. Because the last time he was at the office, he was in the library and Becky came in and . . .

Nope. Not thinking about it.

He tugged on Starr's leash and she started walking ahead of them. Then she must have picked up a scent, because she was off on another grassy detour.

"I'm not thinking about work," he assured his sister, which was true. But also because he wanted to reassure Madison that he was here for her and not half in the office, the way their father always was.

So he should probably get here with her.

"I don't see what's so great about being a lawyer anyway. You guys are always stressed and working crazy hours, but I have no idea what you actually *do* all day."

"Well, we have clients who need us to defend their rights."

"Yeah, like you're such a superhero."

"To our clients we are. When we win. And a Deacon always wins."

"Gag."

"That was a joke."

"You still sounded like Dad when you said it."

An . . . uncomfortable truth.

"I just don't get what's so important that you have to kill yourself over your job. It's not like you're a doctor or, like, saving the world or whatever."

"I think my work is valuable."

"And your clients do."

"Sure."

"That's why they pay you the big bucks."

"Hey, all this genius ain't cheap."

She rolled her eyes. "So, basically, you're trading your life for money."

"I wouldn't say that. I mean, yeah, I make a lot of money . . ."

"But you have no life. All you do is work until midnight, and the only reason you don't work on the weekends is because I've guilt-tripped you out of it. I mean, do you even hang out with anyone besides me?"

"Of course I do," he scoffed, because of course he did. There was Rick—they'd talked about getting a beer one night. When they both weren't working late. And Bullhorn, whom he hadn't seen since the night he met Becky.

And Becky. He saw a lot of Becky.

Mostly that was at work.

He definitely wasn't going to tell Madison about that.

"Starr. I spend a lot of time with Starr."

Madison snorted. Starr just sat in the middle of the trail and stared at them. "I love it when I'm right."

"You're not . . . fine, you're right."

"I just think you either need to save the world or work less."

"I'll take it under advisement."

"And get a girlfriend."

Great. Now his sister wanted him to settle down.

"Seriously. When was the last time you had a girlfriend?"

"Um, I've had plenty of girlfriends. But I lived in New York, so you didn't meet them."

"Wait, you're not working too hard because you don't want to admit you're gay, are you?"

He furrowed his brow at her. What did his work have to do with his sexuality?

"I mean, like, you're not hiding in your work or whatever? Like you're using all of this work time so you don't have to explain your secret sex life."

"Oh. No. I'm not doing that."

"If you were, that would be OK. If you were gay, I mean."

"Thanks."

"Lots of people are gay."

"I know."

"It's not like it was way back in your day."

"Way back in my day? I'm going to let that slide. Anyway, I'm sorry to disappoint you, but I'm not gay."

She shrugged. "Just checking."

"Did Mom put you up to that?"

"Psh. Like I'm going to suddenly start doing what Mom tells me."

"Can't you just try to get along with her?"

"What about Becky?"

If Deacon was drinking a bottle of water, he would have done a spit take.

"What about Becky?"

"Why don't you date her?"

I'd like to, he wanted to tell Madison, but he still had some pride left.

"Why is your dog staring at us?"

"Come on, Starr," he said and tugged on her leash. She walked one step, then sat down again.

"You need to accept the fact that Starr isn't a hiking dog," Madison said. "I don't know why you thought she would be. She's tiny. And look at those perfect, tiny little legs?"

"She did all right at first."

Except now she was sitting in the middle of the trail, staring at him. That Starr stare that he was starting to know so well. The one that said, *I want something from you, and the fact that you aren't giving it to me fills me with contempt and disappointment.*

He had a lot of experience with looks like that.

Finally, Foster just picked her up. She immediately

nestled her little ten-pound body into him and rested her chin on his shoulder.

"Is this what you wanted the whole time?"

Starr didn't say anything, just let out a little old lady dog sigh.

"What a mush baby you are," said Madison and hiked on ahead. Foster followed behind, carrying his dog.

"Oh, speaking of dates. Mom's going to try to get you a date for Thanksgiving."

Ugh. Another reminder of why he was always so busy with work around this time of year. If he was busy, he couldn't get home from New York for Thanksgiving dinner.

"Apparently because you've been back in town, all the sad daughters of her sad friends have been trying to get their hands on you."

"Ugh."

"Thanksgiving's not that far away."

"I know."

"If you found your own date, you wouldn't have to use one of Mom's."

"Starr, will you be my Thanksgiving date?"

Starr licked his cheek.

Madison was right. No matter how many bottles of their favorite wine he brought, if he didn't bring a woman home for her to judge, his mother wouldn't be happy. And if she thought he wasn't bringing a woman for her to judge, she'd bring one of her own.

He needed to bring a date. He scanned through his list of friends. Why wasn't he friends with any women? Why didn't his male friends have sisters he could cajole into being his date? Most of them would be going to their own family Thanksgivings. Maybe he could pay one of the interns to go with him. Would that be a conflict of interest? Ugh, just thinking about it felt wrong.

He shook his head. No. Clearly, no. He couldn't hire a date for Thanksgiving. That would be a new low.

Although seeing the look on his mother's face might be worth it.

No. No. He could do this. He could find someone who didn't have her own family obligations. It would have to be someone who could reasonably pass as his girlfriend. Ugh, and she would really be put through the ringer by his mother. It would have to be someone who owed him a major favor.

Becky.

"You owe me," he'd told her when he'd toted Starr home from the shelter. She'd smiled. She'd agreed.

But would she be available?

She owed him a favor. She'd make herself available.

Chapter Fourteen

"You want me to do what?"

When Foster came into her office and closed the door, that was the last thing she'd expected him to ask her. She didn't know what she'd expected—there definitely wasn't a tiny part of her that fluttered at the idea of being closed in a windowless room with Foster—but this came as a total surprise.

She'd heard him. She just wanted him to repeat it because she didn't believe it.

He let out a weary sigh that was no doubt designed to play on her sympathies. "Would you be willing to pose as my date for my family's Thanksgiving?"

Pose as his date. Not *be* his date. So, despite the flare of annoyance she quickly tamped down, she was safe. She wasn't dating him. Their relationship status would remain safe. Besides, if he kept saying jerky things like *pose as his date*, she would never be in danger of falling in love with him. No matter how great the sex was, she could never love someone she didn't like.

But still. Pose as his date?

"Why?"

"Why what?"

"Why do you need me to *pose* as your date?"

"Uh . . ." He looked uncomfortable. Oh God, wait. Did he think she wanted to actually *be* his date?

"It's an unusual request, that's all I'm saying. I find it hard to believe you can't find your own date."

"Of course I can find a date." Of course he could. She waited.

"Fine, I can't find a date." She smiled. She liked it when he admitted he was wrong. It happened so rarely. Each time was like a tiny little present she kept in her heart.

Not that she kept any part of him in her heart.

"How do you know I don't already have Thanksgiving plans?" She didn't, but she might.

"I don't. That's why I'm asking."

She never had plans for Thanksgiving. She'd always wanted to, but her family thought Thanksgiving was too pedestrian for them. Besides, it involved a lot of cooking. Becky suspected the pedestrianness of it was a convenient excuse to get out of the cooking.

She desperately wanted a real family Thanksgiving. One like Charlie Brown had, or the ones Dakota had. She was always invited to Dakota's family Thanksgiving, but those were in North Carolina and Becky never felt she could impose. It was one thing to drop in on a friend's family across town; it felt like way too much of an imposition to drop in from across the country.

So, really, Foster was presenting the perfect solution. His parents didn't live far away, so it wasn't like anyone would have to pick her up from the airport. She didn't know anyone in the family but Foster and Maddie, but she liked both of them well enough. And, to be honest, she was pretty curious about their parents: How could two people produce such different offspring?

It wasn't like with her and her sisters. She was the only one who was different; all the rest of them were cut from the same cloth. But Foster was competitive and argumentative and a genius. Maddie was like a little foal learning to stand on shaky legs but with a sassy mouth and the ability to cry on command.

It would be really interesting to see their home life. It would be like a sociological expedition. With turkey.

Did she really need to justify it with fake science? She'd always wanted to go to a traditional family Thanksgiving; Foster was handing her the opportunity on a silver platter. Why not take it?

So far she'd taken everything he'd offered—sex, mostly—and it hadn't been all bad. In fact, it had been quite good. Not even quite good. A-plus work. She was beginning to suspect Foster was a sex genius.

Hmm. Would she make an exception to her no-genius rule for a sex genius? It was purely hypothetical of course, because Foster failed in so many other categories of her requirements for her perfect life mate.

"Hello? Becky?"

Right. Foster was sitting in front of her while she inner monologued.

"I don't have Thanksgiving plans, you're right. But I can't just show up at your parents' house, can I?"

"You won't just show up. You'll be with me."

"As your date. Won't they be curious where I came from? Oh, can we create a complicated back-story?"

"If you want to. Or you can just be Becky."

"You're right. And Maddie will be there, right? So I probably can't pretend to be a refugee from another planet."

"That's your backstory?"

"But Maddie will know I'm not a real date. And, wait a second, who brings a date to Thanksgiving? I've never heard of that before."

"My family is weird."

"I don't want weird Thanksgiving. If I wanted weird Thanksgiving, I'd stay home."

He sighed. She felt a victory coming on.

"My mother wants to invite every single daughter of every single one of her friends. Apparently, I'm a catch."

Becky snorted. He ignored her.

"I'm not really interested in dating a girl who

wants to stay in Denver forever and never leave the neighborhood she grew up in, you know?"

"And that's what all your mother's friends' daughters are? Gosh, you really seem to know them well."

"No, I said that badly. I just . . . I don't want to be set up by my mother. She wants me to get serious and settle down. She thinks introducing me to lots of women she approves of will make me see that she's right."

"So I'm not the kind of woman your mother would approve of?"

"That's not what I mean. I just mean that I already know you and I know spending an afternoon with you won't be torture."

"Thanks?"

"I figure it's a win-win. I'll get my mother off my back for at least one day, you'll get to have a big ol' American Thanksgiving."

He had a good point. But she didn't want to seem too eager. Besides, a pretend date seemed dangerous to her. She wasn't sure how. She was in no danger from this guy who was everything she didn't want. He was a lawyer, a genius, and had just admitted to her that he didn't want to settle down. This guy wasn't going to give her the white picket fence of her dreams.

"And you owe me."

And there was that ol' superior look. She was in no danger at all.

Well, he was right. When he'd adopted Starr, both she and Maddie had promised him a favor.

And here was her opportunity to pay her debt. To pay her debt and get the Thanksgiving she'd always wanted.

"Will there be turkey?"

"At Thanksgiving? Of course."

"And stuffing and mashed potatoes and pumpkin pie?"

"Yes. All the normal Thanksgiving stuff."

"And family recipes passed down for generations?"

"Well, no. It's catered."

"Catered Thanksgiving?" That seemed sacrilegious.

"It's too much work, cooking for forty people."

"Oh. That's a lot of food." Forty people? A gigantic Thanksgiving! "Are they all family?"

"Mostly. My two uncles and their kids and grand-kids, some random cousins I see once a year. There are usually a few clients my dad wants to impress. Oh, the neighbors have been coming for the past few years. And then a few of my mom's friends and their single daughters."

A traditional, gigantic Thanksgiving with lots of family and friends. It sounded perfect.

And she did owe him a favor.

And, by posing as his date, she would be doing him a huge favor. Not as huge as adopting a dog he didn't think he wanted, but still . . .

She could pretend to be his date.

What was the worst that could happen?

She could make a fool of herself. As the date of an eligible bachelor, she'd be under pretty serious scrutiny. She'd have to do everything right. And his family . . . from what she knew about the Deacons, this was probably going to be a pretty formal affair. What would she wear? She'd have to study up on forks . . .

"Becky." He put his hand on her arm and she felt the tension seep out of her. "You don't have anything to worry about. I just need a warm body. Nobody's actually going to pay any attention to you."

She was sure that comment was designed to make her feel better. And it did, in a way. She'd get the Thanksgiving she wanted and she wouldn't have to worry about performing well. Foster was such an asshole, he didn't deserve it. And she'd fulfill her obligation to him, so she could be free and clear of him.

"I'm not worried. What time will you pick me up?"

Chapter Fifteen

"Why are you doing this again?"

Becky shoved the hair out of her face with her forearm, then went back to kneading the piecrust. Dakota was sitting on the kitchen counter next to her floury mess, munching on chips while Becky worked.

"Does this look right to you?"

"I don't know," said Dakota. "I've never made it before."

"It's your grandmother's recipe!"

"Yeah, and my grandmother makes it."

"The recipe said don't overmix. Am I overmixing?" She blew that damn strand of hair out of her face.

"I thought you said this dinner was going to be catered."

"Yes," Becky said, squeezing the dough a little more, just to be safe.

"Did he ask you to bring dessert?"

"No, but he's a man. Men don't think about these things."

"You mean men weren't raised with rules of etiquette ingrained in them?"

"Besides," Becky said, ignoring Dakota, "I can't show up empty-handed. His family is inviting me into their home."

"Um, I thought Foster just invited you so he wouldn't have to get a real girlfriend."

"Yes, but his mother doesn't know that."

"True. Although that begs the question: Why do you care what his family thinks of you?"

"I just do, OK?"

Dakota pulled a bobby pin from her pocket and pinned back Becky's errant hair.

Becky sighed. "I'm sorry. I'm just . . . this is my first real Thanksgiving. I can't help being a little anxious."

"You're invited to North Carolina."

"I appreciate that."

"Actually, it would be nice to have someone to navigate the airport craziness with."

"Bullhorn's not going with you?"

"Uh, no. We're not at the meeting-the-families stage yet. Not like you and Foster."

"Ha ha. I'm just a pretend date, remember? Besides—"

"Yeah, yeah, I know. He's a lawyer and a genius and there's no way you'd get involved with him.

Except for three orgasms in the library and a family Thanksgiving."

"That was just . . . that was just sex. This is just Thanksgiving. It's no big deal."

"If it's no big deal, how come you're beating that piecrust within an inch of its life?"

"Oh God, is it too much? Did I ruin it?"

"My grandmother says this pie is impossible to ruin."

Becky picked up the rolling pin. Dakota hopped off the counter, which was good because Becky was going to need all the room she could get. Her kitchen had never felt too small before. When had her kitchen gotten so small?

"Beck."

"I'm rolling."

"Stop a second."

She stopped rolling and turned to face Dakota. Her best friend put her hands on her shoulders, then on her cheeks. "Be careful."

"Why? Am I making the wrong—"

"Not the pie." She poked Becky in the center of the chest.

Becky waved her off. "I'm fine. Really. Really!"

Dakota tilted Becky's head down and kissed her on the forehead. "OK. You'll be great."

"I hope so."

"I wouldn't worry about it. Everyone has a terrible time at Thanksgiving. It's a tradition."

Chapter Sixteen

Driving over to Becky's house, Foster was having serious second thoughts.

He couldn't believe he was doing this. He couldn't believe he was subjecting the perfectly nice Becky to his horrendous family. His horrendous extended family. His mother's judgment would be bad enough, but when she got together with his aunts . . . he was suddenly nervous that Becky wouldn't make it out alive.

"What am I doing?" he asked Starr, who was curled up on the front seat.

Then he remembered that Madison had promised to create a diversion if the heat got too much for Becky. He should probably be concerned about what Madison's idea of a harmless diversion was. And, come to think of it, she hadn't said *harmless*.

Still, she'd smiled when he'd told her Becky was coming. So that was something.

He pulled up to the shabby-looking apartment

complex. This was where she lived? It wasn't terrible—it seemed safe enough—but it was just . . . blah. He'd pictured her living in a quirky, subdivided Victorian or a charming duplex with that white picket fence she was so obsessed about. This looked like crummy student housing. Not her at all.

"What do you think, Starr? It's not too late to turn around." Starr lifted her head, then stood and walked in a circle and settled down facing away from him.

Just when he was starting to question whether he had the right address—he did, he was sure of it, he was just caught off-guard by the unexpected blandness—there was movement on the outdoor stairwell. She emerged, and he was momentarily distracted by her heels and the way they made her legs look . . . long enough to wrap around him. Which was a totally inappropriate thought. This was a fake date. Besides, he already knew her legs wrapped around him.

"This isn't a real date," he told Starr, who ignored him. "It's a favor. It's returning a favor."

Before he could fully convince himself to quit looking at her legs like that, she was opening the car door and handing him something and kissing Starr while he was distracted by her legs climbing into the passenger seat.

"Hi," she said brightly, and he realized she was actually excited about this. She wasn't kidding when she'd said she'd never had a real Thanksgiving. Nobody with firsthand experience of Thanksgiving was this excited about it. Well, he was glad he'd be able to ruin one more illusion for her. It'd be a favor he could do for her.

She buckled her seat belt and Starr settled in her lap as if it were the most natural thing in the world. He wanted to start driving, but he was still holding whatever she'd handed him when she got in.

"Is this a pie?"

She blushed, although he didn't know why. What was embarrassing about pie? It smelled delicious.

"You know my parents have this catered, right?" He was pretty sure he'd told her that. In an effort to ruin more illusions. No wonder she didn't want to date him.

"I know, but it's not polite to show up empty-handed."

"I brought wine." He pointed to his trunk, where the case of wine his mother had asked him to bring was. Not that she could see it.

"Well, most of the wine I drink has a twist off top, so I didn't trust myself to choose something your parents would like."

His parents wouldn't like anything she brought, but that wasn't her fault. And he certainly wasn't going to tell her that.

"Anyway, it's Thanksgiving, and I just felt like baking was appropriate."

He didn't say anything to that. If she wanted to bake, he'd let her bake.

"It smells really good. What kind of pie is it?"

"Sweet potato."

"Sweet potato?"

"Mm-hmm."

"Sweet potato pie?"

"Yes."

"Is it dessert?"

"Have you never heard of sweet potato pie?" She seemed very pleased by that fact.

"Sure I have," he lied. "I've just never eaten it before."

"Oh, good. So you'll have nothing to compare it to."

He handed her the mysterious sweet potato pie. Starr sat up to sniff it, then curled back up on Becky's lap.

"Are you OK?" he asked her. "Do you want me to put Starr in the back?"

"No!" She cleared her throat. "No, she's fine. Her haircut looks good."

"It's grown in a little. She looks a lot less like an exotic rodent now."

"Don't you listen to him," she said to Starr. "You're a beauty queen, no matter what."

Once she figured out how to balance Starr and a pie—the answer was to put the pie on the floor between her feet and keep Starr just where she was—she didn't know what to say. Foster, too, was silent for most of the drive. She imagined he was fuming over the fact that he'd let on that he didn't know something. Not that he'd admitted he didn't know what sweet potato pie was, but she had a feeling the chances of Foster admitting he had any sort of shortcoming . . . well, her parents would throw a big ol' traditional Thanksgiving before that happened.

Well, at least he was pretty to look at.

She could admit that without attaching any deeper feelings to it. Actually, pretty wasn't the right word. Even without the beard, even all clean and polished in his suit—would she ever see him out of a suit again?—pretty wasn't the right word. She wasn't sure what the right word was. Maybe it was because she knew what his face looked like when he was turned on, how his eyes became dark and laser-focused, how his skin flushed when she touched him . . . She should probably stop thinking about how to describe how attractive he was.

She was so absorbed in his jawline that she didn't notice him pulling up to the giant house in tony Greenwood Village. The warm lighting of the entry porch illuminated an impressive stone arch . . . and she knew this wasn't going to be a normal Thanksgiving.

She punched Foster in the arm.

"Hey! What was that for?"

"You promised me a normal Thanksgiving."

"It will be!" He looked confused as he rubbed his arm. Which she thought was a little dramatic. She hadn't hit him *that* hard. She was balancing a pie between her feet and a dog on her lap.

"This isn't the house of a normal family."

He looked through the windshield, as if he'd

never noticed that his parents lived in a friggin' mansion.

"It'll be normal. The caterers make all the traditional foods, there're too many people in the house, obnoxious kids running around, people making passive-aggressive comments . . . all the good stuff."

"All the good stuff," she said skeptically. Too many people? In this house? She didn't think there were that many people in the whole city of Denver.

"All the good stuff and a sweet potato pie." He reached toward her, and for a second she thought he was going to kiss her. But this was a fake date, so there would be no kissing—which was definitely what she wanted—and, besides, he was just leaning in to scoop his dog off her lap.

She carefully retrieved her pie and followed him out of the car and up to the front door.

"We're here!" he shouted to the empty foyer. She was taking in the fresh flowers and the marble table (marble!), when sliding wooden doors parted to reveal a chaotic mix of people—not too many but noisy—and a woman appeared.

"Foster! Hello, love. Oh, and you brought your dog."

"Hi, Mom." Foster pressed a kiss to his mother's cheek and Becky tried not to stare. Foster's mother was . . . she was fabulous. She was tall and tan and wearing a simple sheath dress that looked like it cost more than Becky's rent. Add to that the pearl accessories that sparkled with hidden diamonds and Becky knew she was way outclassed.

Ha. Normal.

"Mom, this is Becky. Becky, this is my mother, Lydia."

"I brought a pie," Becky said, as if Mrs. Deacon couldn't see the pie-shaped dish she was holding.

"Oh, you didn't have to—" Mrs. Deacon looked a little alarmed. "Foster, did you tell her—"

"I told her she didn't have to bring anything. She insisted."

"Oh," said Mrs. Deacon. "Wasn't that kind?"

"It's sweet potato."

"Wonderful! You know, I had the most delicious sweet potato pie on a girls' trip to Savannah."

"It's a family recipe."

"Oh. That sounds delightful."

"Someone else's family. Not mine. My family doesn't eat pie."

"Oh. Well. Thank you. That was . . . Foster, where have you been keeping this delightful woman?"

Foster put his arm around her. But before he could deploy their complicated backstory—which, come to think of it, they hadn't come up with—Lydia turned on her heel and disappeared with the pie.

"You're doing great," he whispered into Becky's ear.

"I don't think she liked the pie," she whispered back.

"She was just surprised. You're fine." And it was the most natural thing in the world for him to pull her a little closer and kiss her on the temple, and it was the most natural thing in the world for her to lean in to him and accept his comfort.

"Son."

Becky would have jumped away from Foster if he hadn't been holding her so tightly. But it wasn't like they were caught making out. And they could totally be caught making out and it wouldn't be a big deal. She was his date.

Not that they'd be making out.

Just that they could.

Oh God, she was nervous.

Foster let go of her long enough to shake the hand of the man who approached him. He was big and barrel-chested, and if Becky was at all curious about what Foster would look like as an older man, there it was, standing in front of her, making a displeased face at Starr.

Good thing she wasn't curious about that.

"Dad. Good to see you. This is Becky."

"Becky, Foster's told us so much about you."

"He has?"

Mr. Deacon cleared his throat. "Please. Call me Andrew."

"Nice to meet you, Andrew."

"And is this your little dog?"

"No, Dad. It's mine. I adopted her. Didn't Madison tell you?"

"Starr is here!"

Madison came charging down the wide, winding staircase and skidded to a stop in front of them. She was dressed pretty much the opposite of her mother: torn jeans, too-big sweater, and big, fluffy socks.

"Starr, my baby, I missed you so much!" She scooped the dog from her brother's arms and received all Starr's grateful kisses.

"Madison, does your mother know you're wearing that to dinner?"

"Yup," she said, and even Becky could tell she was lying.

"Hey, sis."

"Yeah, hi, Foster. Becky! You really came!"

Becky was dislodged from Foster and enveloped in a hug that encompassed Starr as well.

"I brought a pie," she told Maddie, because a teenage girl definitely cared that she was following proper rules of etiquette.

Maddie's eyes lit up. "What did Mom say to that?" she asked Foster.

"She didn't say anything. She loved it."

Maddie snorted. Andrew told Foster he'd "see him for cigars"—whatever that meant—and disappeared back into the room of chaos.

"Is there something wrong with bringing pie?" Becky was sure pie was a totally normal part of Thanksgiving, but the way Madison was acting was causing her to second-guess. How could everything she'd ever read or seen been wrong on that point?

"No, there's nothing wrong with pie," Foster assured her.

"Not for normal people. Mom has a very specific

menu." Maddie stuck her nose in the air. "Carefully curated. She'll be pissed."

"Pissed? Foster! Why didn't you tell me not to bring pie?"

"How could I tell you not to bring pie when I didn't know you were bringing pie? Besides, Maddie's exaggerating. It'll be fine."

She raised her eyebrow at him. Foster had a funny idea of fine.

"Come on," he said, wrapping his arm around her shoulders and leading her into the fray. "Offending the hostess for something you didn't do on purpose is a totally normal part of a Deacon family Thanksgiving. Now let's see what else you've been missing."

Chapter Seventeen

You OK? Foster mouthed across the table at her. At least she thought that was what he mouthed. The flickering candles and the three glasses of wine were making it hard to focus.

She was OK, if that was what he was asking. She was surrounded by cousins and uncles and neighbors and friends from the country club whose names she would never remember. It was so loud she could barely hear the conversation. She'd eaten so much she thought she would bust a seam on her dress.

It was perfect.

"It's snowing!" The shout of one of the many child cousins rang out through the formal dining room, which was impressive because the child cousins were relegated to a table in the parlor.

"Imagine that, snow on Thanksgiving," Grandfather Deacon said, his tone as dry as the white wine.

The woman on her right—the wife of one of Foster's father's most important clients—turned to her and asked, "When's the last time we had snow on Thanksgiving?"

Becky thought about it. It had been a few years. She was about to turn to the woman and tell her that, in the grand tradition of polite small talk, but she was talking to her husband across the table. He was looking at his phone. "Are you looking up the last time we had snow, Timothy?"

Timothy grunted.

Ooo . . . people not saying what they meant but expecting the other person to understand anyway. The elusive passive-aggressive relationship. Now her Thanksgiving was complete. She should have made a bingo card.

Maddie came in to the living room carrying a girl in a pink dress that was all tulle, except for the big wet mess down the front of it. Foster's friend Franny—the one he hadn't been on a date with the other night and who really was just a friend—hopped up and retrieved her messy daughter. Maddie shot her own mother a dirty look and stomped back to the parlor.

Poor Maddie, relegated to the kids' table. But apparently, last year Maddie had sat at the adult table for the first time and took so many sneaky sips from Grandmother Deacon's wineglass that she made a "terrible fuss"—Mrs. Deacon's words—at dessert and then passed out under the table before the dishes were cleared away. So as bad as Becky felt for Maddie, she couldn't really blame Mrs. Deacon for her seating arrangements.

"It's really coming down," said a cousin. No, an

aunt. The new wife of an uncle. Whoever she was, she was wearing a purple feather fascinator and Becky loved her for it.

"But it wasn't supposed to snow today." Mrs. Deacon looked desperately at Mr. Deacon. As if she had consulted the atmosphere and the weather had agreed to knock it off until after dessert. Mr. Deacon didn't seem to be paying attention.

"Whatever happened to that global warming you're always going on about?" a drunk uncle asked Foster's college-aged cousin who Becky was pretty sure was named Tara, but it could also have been Megan or Colleen. Those were all three names that had been bandied about during cocktail hour, but Becky couldn't for the life of her match the face to the name.

"It's climate change, Uncle Gene," said Tara or Megan or Colleen with a very impressive eye roll. "That doesn't mean it's never cold. It means the weather's all wonky."

"We should get going before the roads get bad," said the youngest uncle. (Dave? George? Felix? She had no idea.)

"Since when is snow in Colorado wonky?"

"I'll start getting the kids ready," said the youngest uncle's wife. (Deborah. Becky was moderately sure it was Deborah.)

"But we haven't served dessert yet," said Mrs. Deacon in a tone that, if Becky was less nice, could be described as a whine. "The boys will want their football and cigars first."

"Oh, let them go, Lydia," Mr. Deacon muttered.

"It's wonky when it's unpredictable like this. We were all wearing shorts yesterday."

"Oh, she's a feisty one," said country club dad, who was probably named Chip.

"The thing is, Lydia, I don't want the kids to have all that refined sugar."

"Remember when she was too young to talk? Those were the days."

"Geez, Uncle Gene, don't get mad just because a woman knows more about something than you do."

"A little sugar won't hurt them. It's the holidays."

"Drop it, Lydia."

"Oh, here she goes again, on her little man-hating soapbox. You know, Megan—"

"Megan!" Becky shouted. Yes! That was it! Megan!

Or maybe she hadn't shouted. Megan and Uncle Gene were still arguing over whether she was allowed to be smart, Mrs. Deacon was shooting daggers at youngest uncle's wife's back while she coached her children on giving everyone at the table a kiss good-bye. Becky watched as Foster leaned down to receive a sticky kiss from a towheaded boy in a bow tie. She fumbled for her wine because that hurt her ovaries. He looked up and gave her a quizzical glance. "My ovaries," she explained.

Out loud.

She didn't like being on the receiving end of a glare from Mrs. Deacon.

Real smooth, Becky.

Foster shook his head, but one of the corners of his mouth lifted up in a little smirk. She couldn't decide whether she wanted to smile back or melt into a puddle of shame under the table.

Possibly she was a bit tipsy.

"Kickoff's in ten," said a guy she was fairly certain had not been there before. "We watching in the den, Uncle Andrew?"

"You go on," Mr. Deacon replied. "I'm going to watch the kickoff in my study with a Cohiba. Beautiful dinner, Lydia." He kissed his wife on the cheek, then left the table. Becky wouldn't swear to it, but she thought she saw him snap his fingers and Foster got up, too. Except instead of following his father, he walked around the table—the long way 'round—and leaned over her.

She didn't tilt her head up because she was expecting a kiss. She just did it to hear him better.

"I'm going to my dad's study for a cigar. You'll be OK out here?"

"What? No! Don't leave me here. Your mother hates me."

"No, she doesn't."

"Then why does it look like she's gritting her teeth and staring at us?"

"That's how she always looks on Thanksgiving."

"Yikes."

"My father is much worse."

"Fine, I'll stay here. Preserve the gender dichotomy."

"Good girl."

Before she could tell him that she was *not* a girl, he'd leaned down and kissed her on the lips, just quick, like it was the most natural thing in the world.

When he straightened, he looked as surprised as she felt.

"Becky? Join us in the parlor so Foster can go talk to his father."

She gave Foster a look she hoped conveyed both sympathy and desperation, and prayed his conversation with his father would be short.

Chapter Eighteen

Foster knocked on the door of his father's study and, when he heard his father's "Enter," went in through the open doorway.

His father was behind his giant mahogany desk in his giant mahogany chair, smoking a fat Cuban cigar. Foster bet it didn't taste as good now that they weren't illegal.

He took the seat opposite his father—in a much smaller leather chair—and shook his head to decline the offered cigar.

"Come on, son. It's Thanksgiving. Indulge."

"No, thanks. I'll take some of that whiskey, though."

Without waiting for the answer, he poured himself two fingers in the crystal glass and took a sip. It went down smooth and oaky. Foster would give his father one thing: he knew his whiskey.

"So." Foster leaned back in the lesser leather chair, trying not to wince as it squeaked. "To what do I owe this audience in your lair?"

Andrew Deacon locked his gaze on Foster's. Foster knew the move. He was trying to intimidate him, to stare him down, to make the weaker man blink first.

But Andrew'd been staring guys like him down for a long time. Foster blinked first.

"When are you going to quit dickin' around, son?"

And there it was. Foster showed one sign of weakness, Andrew pounced.

Maybe he should have let Becky come in here with him. She was missing out on a great Deacon family tradition. It was the one where his father berated him for not joining his firm after college and dragging his feet on joining it now, as if it was a foregone conclusion.

"Work's going great, Dad; thanks for asking."

"I hear you're finally stepping up to the big leagues. Congrats on winning the Goliath business. Now you gonna win this case?"

"Yes, sir."

"I know you will, son, because you work hard. You got that from me. And I think it's about time you paid me back."

"For what? For making me genetically incapable of losing an argument?"

"I made you who you are. Your drive, your success, your love of the law: all that comes from me."

"That's right, I keep forgetting you were father of the year."

"We're not going to start this crap again. So I didn't go to your baseball games, boo hoo. Get over it, son. You're almost thirty. It's time you started thinking about putting down roots."

"Putting down roots at your firm?"

"It's only right that I pass it on to you."

"You retiring?"

"Ha."

"No, thanks, Dad. I don't think us working to-gether would be great. Besides, I don't have any experience with mergers and acquisitions."

"You're quick. You'd pick it up. And you have the privilege of being my son, so the others will show you the way."

"Gosh, Dad, practicing a branch of law that doesn't interest me and getting other people to do my work . . . sounds really satisfying."

"I didn't know you were turning into one of those justice warriors, or whatever they are. I seem to recall you working in corporate law, same as me."

"Intellectual property isn't the same as corpo-rate law."

"No, I work for the big dogs, the ones who eat clients like yours for breakfast."

"Jesus, Dad, I'm not getting into a damn pissing contest with you over who has the biggest clients."

"Because you know you don't stand a chance."

Foster went to take a bracing sip of his whiskey, but somehow the glass was empty.

"What do you make of this business with your sister? Don't look so surprised. You're digging your heels in on your career, so I'm changing the subject. What's going on in that girl's brain?"

"I wish I knew."

"She's driving your mother crazy. I'm sick of coming home from work and it's all I hear about. Madison talked back, Madison slammed the door, Madison . . . I don't know, what else does she get into?"

"Dad, she was arrested for underage drinking and public intoxication."

"I know she was. I bailed her out. Your mother was too upset."

"Have you talked to Madison about it?"

"Sure I have. I talk to her plenty. That girl has everything she could ever ask for and she's acting like a damn brat."

Foster clenched his fists and let out a slow breath. He didn't think he was ready to add brawling to the list of Deacon Thanksgiving traditions. Not just yet. Let his father say one more thing about Madison.

"Dad, it's Thanksgiving, so I'm not going to sit here and list all your shortcomings as a father."

Foster was about to launch into a list of just that when the office phone rang.

"Deacon here. Roger! Good to hear from you! I expected you to be knee deep in family bullshit. Ha! Ha! I know. Listen, Happy Thanksgiving; I'm glad you called. Hold on just a sec." Andrew held his hand over the receiver. "I've got to take this, son. Good talk."

Foster left the room in a hurry, more relieved than he was willing to admit.

He needed pie.

* * *

Becky knew it was rude, but she was hoping Foster would beg off dessert. He'd been looking pretty distracted since the talk with his father. Mr. Deacon hadn't emerged from the study yet. She hoped Foster hadn't killed him.

If he had, though, he might be willing to make a getaway.

Thanksgiving was long. Why hadn't anyone ever told her that? And there was so much football! She hated to seem ungrateful for Mrs. Deacon's hospitality, but it was either sit in the parlor and hear gossip about people she didn't know or sit in the den and watch a game she didn't understand. Not even Maddie was there to rescue her because she'd locked herself in her room with her phone and, presumably, Starr.

Instead, Becky sat in a chair near the fire and watched the snow fall.

Besides, she'd brought a pie. It would be rude to leave before she partook of the course she had contributed to, wouldn't it?

Except that when she followed the remaining herd to the dessert table, her homemade sweet potato pie wasn't there.

"Told you," Maddie said, appearing out of nowhere.

"Aren't you supposed to be at the kids' table?" Foster called out as he passed on the way to his seat across from her.

"The snow exodus made some space for me."

"We will *not* talk about the snow," Mrs. Deacon warned from her spot at Mr. Deacon's right hand.

So they didn't. They ate their dessert and talked

about things that weren't snow. And then, when it was time to leave, they couldn't.

They were all staying overnight.

Staying overnight. With Foster.

Gulp.

"Madison, is Starr in there with you?"

As soon as he'd put her down on the marble floor in the foyer, Starr had beat a quick retreat away from all the little kids who thought she was so cute and fluffy. She *was* cute and fluffy, now that her coat was starting to grow back after her post-shelter shave. But the haircut hadn't changed her personality.

Those kids were noisy.

Starr didn't do noisy.

It took them twenty minutes to find her, which wasn't bad, considering the size of his parents' house. She was behind the pull-out sofa in the den, and after two of his uncles moved the thing away from the wall, Madison was able to squeeze behind it and pick Starr up.

It took a while for Starr to allow herself to be put down again. Finally, Madison offered up her room as a dog sanctuary, and after checking on Starr several times and bringing her a small piece of turkey, Foster decided she was happy in there.

But he didn't want her to get too happy in there. Starr was still his dog.

"Yes," came the muffled reply from behind the door.

"Does she have to go out?"

"I just took her."

He waited.

"So is she sleeping in there with you tonight?"

"Can she?"

Foster shook his head. How could he say no? He didn't want Madison to know what a softy he was for that dog.

Hell, she probably already knew.

And Maddie had had to sit through dinner at the kids' table. He could share his dog for one night.

"Fine. Hey, do you have any pajamas Becky can borrow?"

He was tired of talking through the door. Using his rights as the older brother, Foster opened the door to Madison's room without asking first. So even though he'd been talking to her literally seconds ago, she was surprised enough that she couldn't hide the plastic-wrapped brownie behind her back.

"Why are you eating a brownie?"

Starr looked up from her throne on Madison's pillows and let out a soft bark. He gave her a scratch behind the ears.

"I'm not!" She held out the unwrapped but un-eaten brownie and started to stick the plastic wrap back together.

"How are you not stuffed? I feel like I ate enough for three meals." He patted his full, full belly.

"I'm not . . ."

"I saw you eat as much as I did. I don't know where you're putting it . . . wait a second."

Madison wouldn't meet his eye.

"Is that an edible?"

"What do you mean? It's a brownie, of course it's edible."

"You know what I mean."

"Shut up! God, you're such a narc." Her annoyed huff propelled her off the bed and she knelt down and pulled a shoebox out from underneath it.

But before she could slide it back under, Foster grabbed it from her.

"Hey!"

Starr barked at the commotion.

"What other contraband do you have?"

Inside the shoebox was a diary—not interested—some condoms—horrified but not interested—and the brownie. That was it. Not at all as terrible as he was expecting.

He held up a condom and looked at her.

"What? I'm being safe."

"You're sixteen."

"Oh, like you didn't have a girlfriend when you were sixteen."

"We didn't have sex." That was a lie, but he was the older brother. He was allowed to lie.

"Yeah right."

"Anyway, since when do you have a boyfriend?"

"Ugh, I literally cannot talk with you right now!" She flopped down on her bed, face first. Starr got up to sniff her hair, then curled up in a ball next to her ear.

"You know, you have to be twenty-one to consume recreational marijuana."

"Maybe I have a medical card."

"Really? Let's see it."

"I hate you."

He kissed her on the top of her head and handed back the shoebox—sans brownie. "Good night, sister."

"Wait! You can't have that!"

He didn't really want the brownie. Edibles weren't his thing. But he couldn't just leave it with Madison. She was a kid. A kid who was old enough to get busted for public intoxication, but still a kid.

He wondered where she'd gotten it.

He'd grill her about that in the morning.

"Good night, Starr. You traitor." Starr made no move to follow him out the door.

That was fine. He didn't need to sleep with his dog. He'd sleep with . . .

With Becky.

Not *with* Becky of course. But in the same room as her. Because there weren't enough beds for everyone to stay over; well, everyone who was related to the Deacons. The nonfamily guests didn't know any better, so they dared to defy Lydia Deacon and braved the roads. With all the uncles and cousins and aunts, he should consider himself lucky he was only sharing a room with Becky.

A room. Not a bed. They weren't like that.

His back hurt in anticipation of a long night sleeping on the floor.

Maybe he would eat the brownie. Or part of it. Either way, he wasn't leaving it here with Madison.

"It's the price for my silence," he said, and he had the door shut behind him before the pillow she threw at him was even close.

It wasn't until he got halfway down the hallway that he realized he didn't have any pajamas for Becky.

Maybe Becky would sleep naked.

Maybe he needed to eat this brownie and track down another bottle of wine so he would pass out.

When he opened the door to his room—and it was still his room, complete with lacrosse trophies and an unfortunate collection of CDs—Becky was sitting on the bed, her hands tucked under her thighs, her shoes kicked off, and her toes curling into the carpet. He should be grateful she wasn't riffling through his stuff or peeking into the drawers of his nightstand. Good God, what did he have stuffed into the drawers of his nightstand? Instead, he noticed how the hem of her dress had hiked up and she'd taken her hair down.

"Did you—that's not pajamas," she said, nodding toward his hands, which were full of pot brownie rather than of borrowed nightwear.

"Uh . . . she didn't have any clean."

"But she had dessert? Didn't you eat enough dessert?"

"No, this is . . . this is a Colorado dessert."

He watched her face morph from confusion to

understanding. "Ah," she said. "Maddie gave that to you?"

"Not really. I confiscated it."

"Yikes."

"Hey, she's only sixteen."

"I know. That's why I said *yikes*. You're a little tense."

He *was* tense. He felt strung tight as a bow. First he'd caught his sister with drugs—and condoms!—then Becky was going to have to sleep naked, and now that he was sitting next to her he could smell her. She smelled like pie. He wanted to eat her up.

Whoa.

"I might have some old sweatpants or something," he said, hopping off the bed. Anything to keep his back to her.

"Hey, I'm sorry. I didn't mean to poke at a sore subject." Even though she was barefoot on the carpet, he heard her padding up to him, and before he could move away, she put a comforting hand on his shoulder. Well, comforting to every part of him but his groin.

He coughed uncomfortably and bent to his dresser. Oh good. Sweatpants.

"Here," he said, handing one pair to her. "There's the bathroom."

"I know. I was snooping."

Ugh. Tension.

"What? You were gone a long time. But then I started to feel guilty, so I stopped. OK, anyway. I'm babbling. Wine. Pie. You know. Anyway, I'm going to just go in the bathroom to . . ."

He tossed an old T-shirt at her. That was all he needed, her coming out topless.

He swallowed, hard, and turned to look for baggier sweats.

"I can't go out like this," Becky said to her reflection in Foster's childhood bathroom mirror.

The sweatpants and T-shirt he'd lent her were way too long; no surprise, considering how big he was. But he wasn't big, was he? Just tall. And even though he was pretty broad across his chest, the shirt was no match for her and her D-cups. Just like his hips were no match for hers, and she looked nervously at the straining seams of the pants across her butt. She didn't used to think her butt was that big. Foster was making her reconsider.

No, he wasn't. His pants were. Foster liked her ass, and she liked the way he grabbed handfuls of it when she was . . .

Now you definitely can't go out like this. Because now, in addition to what she assumed was his high-school logo being stretched beyond recognition, it also had two little pebble points where her nipples were hardening at the thought of her riding Foster . . .

"Quit thinking about it," she hissed. Why was she so bad at listening to herself?

She stuck her arms inside the shirt and pressed her elbows out in a desperate attempt to give herself a little breathing room. It might ruin the shirt, but she didn't care.

Desperation made her not very nice.

Shirt stretched, she washed her face with the random products she found under the sink—she wouldn't be getting any pimples tonight!—but she didn't see a spare toothbrush. She briefly considered the one sitting in the cup next to the sink. But no. She couldn't. She wasn't that not-very-nice, and besides, she didn't know how long that toothbrush had been sitting there. So she squirted a little toothpaste on her finger and did her best.

"OK," she said to her reflection. She sucked in a big breath, then whooshed it out. "No more big breaths," she told her reflection, then reached in her shirt to stretch it out again. At least the too-long shirt covered the worst of the tight sweatpants.

Without a deep breath, she opened the bathroom door.

And gasped.

No amount of shirt stretching was going to hide the deliciousness of Foster's naked butt.

He must have heard her because he turned. Then he must have realized that turning gave her an even more indecent view, so he turned back. But he must have forgotten that he had one foot in the leg of his sweatpants, because he went down—hard—on the other side of the bed.

"Are you OK?" She wasn't laughing. She really wasn't laughing.

She was totally laughing.

"Don't come over here!" he shouted from the floor. There were the sounds of some mad fumblings, then he popped up, all his bits and pieces covered by a pair of plaid pajama pants that actually fit.

Too bad.

No, no, she scolded herself, thinking of her too-tight shirt. *Not too bad at all. Very good.*

"Those, uh . . ." He cleared his throat. "Are you comfortable?"

"Yup," she said, resisting the urge to crawl under the bed and hide.

The bed.

Oh.

How was that going to work?

He must have caught her looking pillow-ward because he grabbed one of the pillows and the plaid throw at the foot of the bed. "I think I'll sleep on the floor, if that's OK?"

"Sure yeah. Sure, that's OK. Yeah." *Sure, fine, if the idea of me busting out of your old clothes doesn't turn you on, fine, go ahead and sleep on the floor.*

Oh God, was she turning into his mother? Saying things she didn't mean and expecting him to understand her anyway? "Are you sure you'll be comfortable?" Because the way she thought of him definitely wasn't motherly.

"No problem. I'm ready to pass out. I've eaten so much."

"And drunk so much."

"Ha, yeah, no. I mean, I drank enough. Are you sure it's OK that we're staying here? I'm an adult.

My mother can't actually require me to stay the night."

"It's fine. Really. I've got these nice sweatpants on . . ."

"Sorry about that. I was really skinny in high school."

She gave him a moment to let the way that sounded sink in.

"Not that you're not skinny! I mean, you're not, you're . . . you have womanly . . . rgh." He quit fumbling and backpedaling when he saw her laughing at him.

Laughing made her shirt feel tighter and that made his pants look tighter, and for one hot second she thought he was going to launch himself across the room and devour her.

"Well, good night," he said suddenly and firmly. Then he was on the floor, blanket tossed haphazardly over him.

"Good night," she said, and she crawled under the covers. Alone.

Whose stupid idea was it to sleep on the floor?

Not his. If he had his way, he'd be sleeping in bed with Becky.

Not that she'd told him not to sleep in bed with her.

Because he could totally sleep in the same bed with her and keep his hands to himself.

It wasn't like the sight of his summer lacrosse

camp shirt straining across her breasts made her look completely and totally hot. No, that was ridiculous.

His back hurt.

He was never getting to sleep.

He wasn't lying earlier. He had eaten way too much; it was as much a tradition on Thanksgiving as football and trying really hard not to talk about politics. But it wasn't making him tired. Or, rather, it wasn't making him tired enough to get the image of Becky's ass in those sweatpants out of his head.

She moaned and shifted in her sleep and the sheets rustled around her.

He bunched his hands into the blanket.

He sat up and looked at the clock radio. It was only one A.M. He had a long damn night ahead of him.

Then, in the green glow of the clock radio, he spotted Madison's brownie.

On one hand, the thought of eating anything else made his stomach hurt.

On the other hand, he needed to relax. And it was either spend the night jerking off in the bathroom or take a more medicinal approach to relaxation.

He got up quietly.

He unwrapped the brownie.

"Foster?"

Becky's voice was husky with sleep and it went right to his groin.

He shoved a chunk of brownie in his mouth.

"Are you eating?"

She sounded husky and confused.

"Mm-hmm," he said with a mouthful of brownie.

"Are you eating your sister's pot brownie?" She sat up, and the comforter fell back, revealing his high-school wet dream. A hot girl in his T-shirt.

He groaned.

"It's that good, huh?" When he finally convinced his gaze to move to her face, he saw she had one eyebrow raised. And her hand out.

He broke off a piece and gave it to her.

"Um," she said. "God, now maybe I can sleep."

"You weren't sleeping before?"

"No, I was too . . ." She cleared her throat. "I was too full."

"I was hoping this would help me sleep." He held up the brownie, or what was left of it. He offered her another piece. She shook her head.

"You know, this isn't going to kick in for a while."

He wrapped up the rest. He'd give it to . . . well, he didn't know what he'd do with it. Maybe Grandmother Deacon could use it.

"It's only one o'clock?" Becky flopped back against the pillows. "This night is going to last forever." Then she pulled the covers back. "Quit standing over me."

"I . . . uh . . ." How do you tell a woman that you'd like to sit next to her, but your giant erection is going to make it embarrassing?

"Relax, I'm not going to jump on you."

Not what I was worried about.

But the floor sucked, so he crawled under the covers and lay down next to her.

"So," he asked, putting his hands behind his head. "How was your first Thanksgiving?"

"Great. Amazing." She leaned up on one elbow. "Thank you."

He leaned up on an elbow to face her. "Thank *you.* My mother barely mentioned eligible women who might need dates to various holiday parties."

She flopped her head forward and laughed.

When she tossed her head back, she was smiling wide and her hair was all over her face. He didn't know why he did it. He'd sworn he wouldn't. But he traced his finger across her forehead and tucked her hair behind her ear. She sucked in a breath. He ran his finger along her cheek. Across her lips. Under her chin. Tilted her face up.

She was the one who closed the space between them. She was the one who pulled him nearer, who opened his mouth wider so her tongue could get inside. She was the one who wrapped her arms around her shoulders and pulled so their bodies were aligned, then threw her leg over his hip and got them even closer.

He was pretty sure his high-school sweatpants were destroyed in their frantic efforts to get them off, but he didn't give one iota of a shit. He just wanted her naked and close, and when he shifted them so she was underneath him, he rolled his hips into hers and she gasped at him and he rolled again and she dug her nails into his shoulders and closed her eyes tight.

How did she do that? How did she manage to make him feel like a god when she wasn't even look-ing at him? The way her body reacted to his . . . he felt like a king. Like king of the goddamn world.

He hooked an arm under her knee, pulled her leg up to his shoulder. God, his librarian was flexible. He flexed into her again and she made a sound he'd never heard before. Part growl, part squeal, part laugh. He wanted her to do it again. But when he shifted into her again, her whole body bowed up tight and her arms went wild until he grabbed one and she fisted his hair and gasped desperately in her release. It had happened so fast, he'd barely had time to savor it. He wanted to watch her writhe and catch her breath, and then he wanted to see if he could do it again, but it was too late. He shuddered and growled and he felt her limp arms go around his back as he jerked and then, finally, relaxed.

"You are so much more comfortable than the floor."

She laughed, even though she'd thought she was too tired to laugh. She didn't know if it was the brownie or Foster, but her limbs felt heavy and she felt all floaty and relaxed.

Foster ran his fingers up and down her bare arm. She shivered.

"Are you cold?"

Before she could answer, he'd pulled the covers up over them both and rubbed her back.

"I think you killed me," she said softly into his chest. He tipped up her chin and kissed her gently, then a little less gently. Then, before she could tell him that, while his kisses were delightful, she didn't have the energy to lift her limbs, he let his head flop back onto the pillow.

"Becky."

"Mm." He started stroking her scalp. She wanted to purr, but she was too tired.

"What are we doing?"

"Sleeping?"

"No, I mean . . . I mean this." He squeezed her shoulder.

She tipped her head up, rested her chin on his chest. "I can't date you."

"Why not?"

"I'm supposed to be using you for your body."

"Thanks?"

She reached up and ran a finger along his jaw, where the stubble was coming in. "If we started dating, would you grow a beard again?"

He raised his eyebrow at her. "I don't know. It's not very professional."

"Mr. Glassmeyer has a beard."

"Mr. Glassmeyer is almost seventy and he's a founding partner. He can do whatever he wants."

She sighed. "Okay. How about if you don't shave on the weekends?"

"Deal."

She smiled sleepily and put her head back on his chest.

Had she just gotten herself a boyfriend?

"Are you sure about this?" her boyfriend asked.

"No. But that's OK."

"Why? Because I'm a lawyer?"

"Not really."

"Because I'm a genius?"

"Because you won't shut up."

He growled at her and surged them both up, tickling her ribs. She squealed and flailed, but he let her pin him underneath her. They lay there, panting, bodies aligned, his arms held up over his head. She leaned down and kissed him, a little deeper than she meant to, and his arms went around her and he rolled her onto her back and good thing she wasn't tired because they weren't getting any sleep tonight.

Chapter Nineteen

It wasn't so bad, dating a genius.

Dating a lawyer kind of sucked, but only because Foster worked so many hours. That was okay, though, because it gave her an excuse to let herself into his apartment so she could walk his dog. She and Starr were getting to be besties. Starr only barked for a minute when she came over without Foster. The first time she'd done it, it had lasted half an hour. She didn't think her eardrums would recover. Or that his neighbors would forgive her.

Sometimes she took a shower. That shower was a thing of beauty. High-rise living might not be her style, but she could appreciate its benefits.

Sometimes he'd text her to say he was leaving work and she'd jump in the shower then, so when he got home, if he wanted to say hello to her, he had to get into the shower with her. It was the only way.

Plus, living in a high-rise, they could leave the curtains open all the time and watch the lights of

Denver twinkle on and off while they watched a movie.

She and Maddie were getting closer, and that was fun. Becky was an older sister, but she'd never gotten the chance to actually *be* an older sister; Miranda had it all figured out before Becky did. Tying her shoes, riding a bike, eating with a spoon. Not in that order. Becky did learn to read first, but that was about the only way she excelled.

But with Maddie, it wasn't a competition. Maybe it was because their age gap was so wide, or maybe it was because no one called her "Maddie's older sister," like they had in middle school. And grade school. And high school.

Not in that order.

Maddie'd finished her community service and her parents were giving her her license back, and the keys to her car, as long as she followed their strict rules. Becky and Foster were the victims of many angry eye rolls when they sent Maddie home so she could make curfew, but she was doing OK. They even had Dylan—who really was a girl—over for pizza and a movie.

It was a high-rise, sure, but it was all very cozy.

She should have known it wouldn't last.

Chapter Twenty

It was a Saturday afternoon, the first one warm enough to go outside without a jacket. It seemed like the whole city was on the Bluffs loops, walking their dogs and their kids and soaking up the sun. It was an easy hike, and one that Foster had taken Starr on before.

Becky didn't really know what hiking with Starr entailed. She didn't think such an avid sleeper would be into the three-mile loop, but she didn't question Foster when he picked her up and told her their destination.

Then they got to the parking lot and she realized how Starr managed to cover so much trail.

She rode in a backpack.

It was specially designed for dogs, Foster explained once Becky stopped laughing. Then he put Starr in the pack and strapped her on and Becky lost it again. What was she supposed to do? This tall, muscly, scruffy guy—because he kept his promise not to shave on the weekends—in hiking shorts with a fluffy white head sticking out over his shoulder, sniffing the mountain air.

He also had a leash dangling from the pack because once some jerk on a horse had yelled at him for having his dog off leash. And even though Foster, as one of the foremost legal minds in the state, could have won the argument that, because Starr was in a backpack, she was restrained and therefore he was following the spirit of the law, he let it go and walked with a leash slapping against his leg.

It was dangerous, watching this handsome man take such care with a fragile creature. It made her think he would take just as much care with her heart. But she was still afraid. None of her other perfect boyfriends had worked out before, and, even though he'd started out all wrong, Foster was turning out to be the most perfect of them all. She knew when the other shoe fell, this one was really gonna hurt.

And no amount of anonymous lumberjack sex would reset her after this.

But that was for later. For now, she just took Foster's hand and hiked while Starr snoozed on his back.

Then, later, after they'd stopped at a brewery for a burger, she went with him to his apartment and he fed the dog and started the shower and they soaped each other up and fell into bed, wet and exhausted.

She was a goner.

* * *

Foster jerked awake. He was having an anxiety dream about Claire calling him in the middle of the night to tell him that all their papers were scattered all over the floor of the library.

But it wasn't a dream. It was his real phone.

He really hoped it wasn't Claire.

"Hmph," Becky said as he dislodged her from his shoulder to answer. He looked at the screen. It wasn't work. It was Madison. Which was much worse than work.

Then he heard Becky's phone ring, and her phone never rang after nine. Despite a complete lack of practice, she was faster than he was.

"What? Dakota, slow down, I can't understand you."

He picked up his call. "Madison? What's going on?"

"I fucked up."

Chapter Twenty-One

Becky didn't trust herself to speak on the drive over to the shelter. She wasn't mad at Foster specifically, but she couldn't shake the feeling that this was his fault. It wasn't. Of course it wasn't. As a concession to her irrationality, she let him keep his hand on her knee as he drove. She covered it with her own hand, squeezed. Because he was just as pissed and tense as she was.

Madison, in her infinite teenage wisdom, had wanted to show her friends where she'd been doing her community service, so she'd broken them in to the shelter. She wanted to throw a party for the dogs.

The kids were drunk. And stoned. And really annoying, according to Dakota, but that was secondary to their actual criminal behavior.

As they pulled in the driveway, she only saw one car there. It must have been Bullhorn's, because that was who she saw wrestling a much taller guy out the front door and onto the nearest bench. She saw him point and give him a *stay*, and the guy sat there with his head hanging down.

Foster was out of the car almost before he put it in park. He charged past Bullhorn—Becky doubted he even recognized his old friend—and was in the shelter before she had the car door closed.

"What happened?"

"Stupid kids tore the place up. This asshole was getting into the Puppy Chow."

"I'm hungry," the asshole whined.

"You've got the munchies, asshole. It'll pass."

"How's Dakota?"

"As of three minutes ago, I was pretty confident her rage had cooled down from murderous to just maiming levels. Then this asshole wouldn't keep his trap shut, so I figured it was safer for me to get him away from Dakota than it was for me to hang around inside."

"You want me to sit outside and watch him?" she offered.

"Nah. I've got his keys. He can run if he wants to; he won't get far."

The asshole had slumped over onto the bench and started snoring.

Bullhorn shrugged and Becky followed him inside.

Inside was a mess.

There were streamers all over the reception area, pens and markers and scissors all over the floor. Becky climbed over the detritus back to the cages, where Maddie was sitting on the floor with another guy and a girl, the three of them stifling giggles while several loose dogs chowed down on the spilled kibble everywhere.

Dakota and Foster were next door, struggling to attach a wire door to one of the cages. A few others hung open and looked beyond repair.

"Babe, come on." Bullhorn took Dakota's place, and together he and Foster muscled the door back onto its spring-mounted hinges.

"You OK?" Becky asked Dakota.

Dakota wiped her eyes. "Other than being so angry I could murder those . . . they wanted to let all the dogs out."

"What? Did they?"

"No, thank God. Bullhorn and I got here just as they were letting them out of their cages. The tall one managed to break a couple of the doors. *Because animals shouldn't be caged up,* he said. As if this is a fucking animal research facility! These are fucking homeless dogs!"

Becky rubbed Dakota's arms and she took a deep breath. "Sorry. I'm pissed. I think I scared Foster."

"He'll be OK. What did Maddie say?"

Dakota snorted. "As soon as I realized I wasn't getting a coherent word out of her, I told her and her friends to stay the hell out of my way."

"Why is there food everywhere?"

"Oh, you didn't hear? It was also a birthday party, so they opened five twenty-pound bags of kibble and spread it all over the floor, then let the dogs go to town. So now, after we get the cages fixed, I'm going to have to walk twenty-seven dogs."

"I'll stay and help."

"Thanks. Let me take a couple of them out now. Can you sweep up the other room?"

Becky gave Dakota a big squeeze, then let her go take care of business.

"I'm going to take Maddie home," Foster told her. "Do you mind hanging out here? There isn't enough room in the car for all of them and you."

"Sure. I told Dakota I'd help for a while. And you and Maddie probably need some time to talk."

He snuffed out a humorless laugh. "Did you see her in there? There's not going to be any talking to her tonight. I'll let her crash at my place and she can face Andrew and Lydia tomorrow."

"Oh."

"What? I can see you're thinking something. Just tell me."

"I thought you were trying to be a positive influence on Maddie."

He arched his eyebrow at her. "Are you saying this is my fault?"

"No! No, but . . . if you just drop her off at your parents', they're not going to do anything. It just seems like . . . like you guys are actually letting her get away with all this."

"And what do you suggest we do instead?"

"Hold on, no. I'm not going to try to tell you what to do. It's just . . . I know Maddie a little, and I know what it's like to be a teenage girl. She's going to keep pushing and keep screwing up if she doesn't think anyone cares that she keeps screwing up."

"Of course I care. I had to come out here in the middle of the night when I could have been having sex with my girlfriend. Instead, I'm picking up my stoned sister while my girlfriend tells me how I should handle her."

"I'm not—"

"You probably shouldn't be the one giving out advice on how to deal with sisters, you know."

Ouch. That one stung. "It's not about me . . ."

"Exactly."

"Foster—"

"Listen, I'm really pissed right now and I'm going to say something I'll regret . . ."

"Like what? Like I have a fucked-up family so I have no place having a *conversation* with my boyfriend?"

"Yeah, and like how you should mind your own damn business. I'm dealing with it, Becky."

"Like the way you dealt with finding her with drugs on Thanksgiving? By patting her on the head and pretending it didn't happen?"

"I wasn't the only one who ate that brownie."

"Look, I know you love your sister and you want to be a friend to her because she feels alone in the world, but you're letting her off the hook here. At the very least you're coddling her, but at the worst, you're enabling her."

"I'm enabling her? Really. By being here for her when she gets in trouble?"

"No, by not making her face the consequences. What if one of the dogs had bitten someone? What if one of her friends, I don't know, climbed onto a rock and cracked their skull open? What if the cops had showed up? Would you just take her home and put her to bed?"

"I said I would deal with it."

"She needs help, Foster. Like, real help."

"Thank you. I've got it from here."

The sounds of three messed-up teenagers singing a barely recognizable pop song drifted in from the next room, accompanied by a variety of dog howls.

If Becky wasn't so tense, she'd make a joke about how Maddie was a worse singer than he was.

Foster ran his hand through his hair in that frustrated way he had. "I better get them out of here before Dakota kills somebody."

She nodded and watched him go. She heard him dragging Maddie out of the shelter and assumed the other two followed. Her heart went out to him, really it did. But he was right. This wasn't her family to deal with. She needed to mind her own business. She went in search of a broom.

Chapter Twenty-Two

Foster was a coward.

Only cowards ate their lunch at their desk instead of trying to work things out with their girlfriends. Sure Becky had called him on Sunday to make sure Maddie was OK—physically OK, pissed as hell at him—and to say that she'd give him some space while he dealt with his family stuff. Which wasn't what he wanted, and he told her so.

So instead of answering his mother's calls and going out to see his sister, he spent all day Sunday in the office, just like the soulless workaholic Madison had accused him of being.

And now he was sending Kevin out for his lunch. He tried to tell himself that that didn't make him like his father. There was a big difference between doing business on Thanksgiving and asking someone to bring you lunch.

Right?

"Come in," he said to the sound of the knock on

his door. "Just put it on the conference table, Kevin. I'll get to it in a minute. Thanks."

"Who's Kevin?"

He looked up. That wasn't Kevin.

It was Becky's sister. The genius one, Miranda.

"Foster, right?"

"Yeah, hi. We met a while back at Razor. Nice to see you again, Miranda."

"You're working on that case for Goliath, right? The one about the glyphosate herbicides?"

He'd filed the documents, so it was a matter of public record. Still. Why was Becky's sister in his office talking to him about it?

She worked with chromosomes, right? He tried to remember their conversation at Razor. Then he remembered that she'd said it was too complicated for him to understand.

"You know, finding an effective herbicide that's apian-friendly will have ripples of benefit throughout the entire ecosystem."

Foster felt a headache coming on.

"So it's for the public good, to be able to study Goliath's chemistry."

"Miranda, I really can't discuss the case with you."

"Why not? I'm the one who headed up the project at CoLabs."

Forget a headache. Foster felt like his whole brain had just exploded.

"Miranda, you *really* can't be in here." He stood up to usher her out, but she didn't budge from her chair. Instead, she looked around his office, as if noticing for the first time that the room had walls.

"Doesn't my sister work here?"

He was going to have to call Security. Except if he called Security, there would be no way to sneak her out of the building without anybody knowing.

Stupid geniuses.

Miranda turned in her chair and looked at his closed office door.

"I didn't see her when I walked in."

"Becky? She doesn't sit out there. Her office is in the library."

"Her office? Oh."

"Did you think she was my secretary?"

Miranda just shrugged. How gross must she think he was, bringing over a bottle of wine to his secretary's family dinner?

Come to think of it, he'd seen his father do exactly that.

His headache was back.

"You're dating her, right?"

Miranda wasn't saying much, but he was still having trouble keeping up with her. At least she wasn't talking about herbicides.

"Am I dating Becky?"

"Yeah."

"I thought you guys didn't speak."

"We don't, really. We don't, like, hate each other. We just . . . we're on different planes."

Foster did his very best not to roll his eyes.

"Hm. I've never met anyone Becky's dated before."

"Well, you shouldn't be meeting me now."

She squinted her eyes and tilted her head. He

knew that look. Starr gave him that look when she was trying to figure out what the hell he was doing.

"You know, my sister's pretty great."

That wasn't what he was expecting. But he wasn't too shocked to agree. "I know."

"We have a weird family."

"I know that, too."

"Becky doesn't fit in, but I think that's because she's the only one of us who's not a shitty person."

Whoa. Something else he wasn't expecting.

"I'm sure you're not—"

Miranda held up her hand, and he was pretty grateful he didn't have to finish his lie. "I'm a scientific genius, but I'm not unaware of my shortcomings as a sister."

Foster leaned back in his chair, conflict of interest forgotten. This was going to be interesting.

"Do you think I didn't know how much it hurt her growing up as 'Miranda's big sister'? Well, I didn't. I was the smartest kid in my class; who wouldn't want to be associated with me? And she didn't have a problem being 'Astrid's little sister.' At least I don't think she did. I don't know, nobody ever called me that. I was always just Miranda."

"What's your point, Miranda?"

"Well, it turns out she did hate it. She told me once. She shouted it in my face, and then we never talked about it again. It took me a while to figure out why. I think it's because it made her feel like she had to be competitive when she isn't a competitive person at all."

He knew that. She'd let him win every argument

they'd ever had. Including the one when he was a total ass and told her to butt out of his business.

"I also know that the only time she ever got in trouble in school was when she gave Brad Prescott a black eye for saying I was weird."

Foster couldn't picture Becky punching anyone. Then he thought about her defending something she loved and he could sort of see it.

"Anyway, I hope you guys are really happy. She deserves it."

"Thanks. You're right."

"And if you hurt her, I'll give you a Prescott."

"Noted. You should probably leave my office."

She did, but it didn't make what he had to do any easier.

It was almost a relief to be back at work. That was how chaotic her weekend had been.

Not the whole weekend. Just Sunday. Spending the day with Dakota had given her emotional whiplash. First Dakota was angry at Maddie and her stunt, then Becky would comfort her and Dakota would transfer her anger to Foster, who'd left Becky in some kind of limbo between a fight and a breakup. It didn't help that her brief text conversation with him seemed to indicate that he'd spent all of Sunday at work.

Becky tried to be understanding. His family situation was a big thing, and the case was a big thing. He had a lot of big things to juggle.

Bullhorn offered to kick his ass, which made

Dakota feel better, but Becky didn't see how adding physical injury to Foster's list of things to juggle was going to help her in any way.

So, yeah. Work was much less complicated.

"Ugh, Monday, amirite?"

Will sauntered into her office and plopped, un-invited, into the chair across from her desk. He tilted it back on two legs and pulled a fluffy pom-pom pen out of the front pocket of his shirt.

"Why is the weekend so short?" Will asked her. She didn't have an answer for that. This weekend had felt like the longest of her life. "Oh, hey, I heard some kids broke into the New Hope shelter over the weekend."

Great. Work was supposed to be a refuge from her personal life.

Wait, was it? That didn't feel right. Ugh, she'd make a terrible workaholic.

Her phone pinged. A text message from Foster, asking her to dinner. She wished her heart didn't give a little leap of hope at that. He was probably going to break up with her or something.

She needed to call Dakota.

Dakota had enough on her plate.

"Whoa, who's that?"

Will and his pom-pom pen got up to talk to who-ever had just entered the library. "Yeah, her office is back there," she heard him say, but she was too busy trying to decide if she could bother Dakota with her concerns about dinner to pay much attention.

"The lawyers' offices are much nicer."

If Becky didn't have such a headache, she would have had to pinch herself to make sure she was awake. What was Miranda doing in her office?

"Hi." She stood up and offered Miranda Will's now-vacated chair. "What are you doing here?"

"This is pretty nice. I wasn't expecting you to have an office."

"Miranda . . ."

"Did you know your boyfriend is suing me?"

"He is? What?"

"Well, he's representing Goliath, who's trying to block my work on making glyphosate herbicides safe for bees."

Becky's first reaction was *ugh, that was the big intellectual property case everyone was so worked up about?* But then what Miranda said sank in.

"Miranda, are you trying to get me to influence the case in some way?"

"What? No! Can you even do that? I thought you were just a librarian."

Well, that was a nice vote of confidence.

"We were talking to the CoLabs lawyers about our research—they didn't get it—when someone mentioned they were going to have a tough case against Foster Deacon at Polak and Glassmeyer, and I was like, I know that name."

"Oh God."

"So I stopped by to see if I could talk to him about it. The CoLabs counsel didn't seem to care about the science, only the particular formula of herbicide we were testing. I tried to explain that glyphosate is fairly generic but the Goliath brand—"

"Miranda. Stop." Becky took a deep breath. "You need to stop talking to me about this."

"Oh, so you do have influence?" There was no venom behind Miranda's question, just genuine curiosity. *Oh, you're a productive member of society? That's kind of surprising, given your far inferior intellectual abilities.*

Ha. And Foster said she couldn't deal with her own family stuff.

"No, Miranda, I don't have influence. But there's such a thing as ethics."

"You guys have ethics, too?"

Becky let out a slow, calming breath. "I don't work on the actual cases per se. I'm not privy to the specifics."

"Huh."

"It's not my job to argue the case. I'm not a lawyer."

But she had an idea of what Foster wanted to talk to her about over dinner. It probably wasn't that he'd had a change of heart and wanted her to be a part of every aspect of his life, and also that he was buying a house with a white picket fence and would she consider moving in there with him?

She should have stuck to her rules. No lawyers. Nothing but hot lumberjack sex. And definitely don't get to know them afterward because where had that ever gotten her?

"Becky?"

Miranda was still there. What was Miranda doing there? Oh right, potentially sabotaging Foster's case and marveling at how little work her sister actually did.

"I'm sorry, Becky."

Before she could ask Miranda what she meant, she was out the door.

Becky had been waiting a long time for someone in her family to acknowledge the way they belittled her and devalued her and messed with her self-esteem. She supposed this was the best she was going to get.

That was okay, she decided. The power of her righteous indignation would help her be strong when she let Foster off the hook.

Can't do dinner.

Tomorrow?

Miranda came by. Said she saw you too.

Yeah. About that . . .

Don't worry, I told her I can't help her. And even if I could help her, I couldn't, you know?

Not sure. But thank you.

Is it a problem that my sister is involved in this case?

Not technically, no.

But in a vague, nontechnical way? Don't lie.

Yes. Potentially. It could look bad.

Maybe we should chill out for a bit.

Chill out?

Take a break. You're dealing with a lot and I don't want to cause trouble for you here.

Just a break, right?

Sure.

I appreciate that. Starr will be disappointed.

Becky?

Becky?

Chapter Twenty-Three

Becky was grateful for the silent mode on her phone that let her ignore Foster's messages, and for her sympathetic boss, who took her story of her impending migraine at face value and let her go home. And she was grateful that Dakota wasn't home when she got to her house so Becky could cry in the driveway in peace. And she was grateful that when Bullhorn came outside to see what she was doing, he didn't ask her any questions, just let her inside and gave her a beer and told her Dakota was on her way.

"He did what?" Dakota said when she got home and Becky told her the whole story. She was grateful for Dakota's righteous indignation on her behalf, too, however misplaced it was.

"He didn't do anything. He just agreed to what I suggested. That we take a break until things cool off."

"Because your sister, with whom you have no relationship, is involved in this case he's working on?"

"Not just that. He's also dealing with a lot with Maddie—"

"Pfft. Maddie."

"He told me that he moved back here for two reasons. One was this job at P and G and the other was Maddie. I'm not going to be the one who gets in his way."

"Yes, because there's no reason why you should have the person you're in a relationship with be involved in your personal drama."

"I don't want to be involved in his personal drama. I just want a nice, quiet boyfriend who—"

"Wait. No. Uh-uh. I thought we were done with that. No more boring guys for you."

"I'm on my second beer and it's barely five o'clock on Monday. I'll take boring and normal."

What did Dakota know about her relationship problems? Dakota had no relationship problems. She and Bullhorn sat next to each other on the couch, listening across the coffee table as Becky explained why she should never have listened to Dakota in the first place, looking awfully cozy together. Or as cozy as two people could look in these circumstances.

What the hell was going on with the world?

"I should go," she told the happy couple. "Sorry, you don't need to . . . I just needed to let it out . . . I'll just . . ."

"Beck, stay." Dakota gently pushed her back into the oversize chair. "I'll make you tea."

Becky nodded. She could use some tea. And some whiskey.

Tea first.

She saw the panicked look that crossed Bullhorn's face. She felt bad for the guy.

"So . . ." he said, slapping his hands on his thighs. "Uh. Wow. Your day sucks, huh?"

Becky gave a watery laugh. "That's one way to put it."

"You want I should kick Deke's ass?"

"That's the second time you've offered to do that."

"I'm a good friend."

"I know. Thank you, but no."

Bullhorn looked relieved. "Good. I'm pretty sure Deke would whip me."

Becky didn't agree, at least not out loud.

"I would've done it anyway."

"That's what you need," Dakota said, putting a steaming mug in front of Becky.

"For Foster to get his ass kicked?"

"No."

"For Bullhorn to get his ass kicked?"

"No. But you need someone who'll offer to fight a much bigger guy who'll definitely inflict severe bodily pain on him."

"Thanks, babe."

"I love you, but it's true. And I love you for standing up for Becky. Because Foster won't."

"It's not a matter of standing up, Dakota. I'm not

going to mess up the two biggest things in his life just so I can have a boyfriend."

"I thought you said this was just a break."

"It is. I'm giving him space to deal with his family, and it just happens to coincide with other professional benefits."

"Benefits for him. What about for you?"

"Dakota."

"Let me ask you a question. You want a normal relationship, right?"

"Yes! God, that's all I've wanted this whole time!"

"What's a normal relationship? One where people never fight?"

"No. We're not fighting anyway."

"You should be fighting. You shouldn't be letting him roll over you when he can't handle his life."

"That's just how it is. He's got a high-pressure job. I shouldn't have gotten involved with him in the first place. I need a normal guy with a normal family so I can have a normal life."

"OK, let me try this out. Normal family. That's mom and dad—"

"Normal doesn't mean heteronormative."

"Fair enough. There's a loving pair of irrelevant gender designation, some kids—"

"Kids are optional to a normal life."

"OK, maybe there are kids."

"But if there are kids, they're showered with love."

"But not too much love that they think it's OK to trash an animal shelter when they're stoned."

"I don't think Maddie did that out of an excess of love."

"Right. Fine. Just the right amount of love. And this nongender-specific pair with or without kids live in a nice house with a white picket fence . . ."

"The fence is just a metaphor. They could live anywhere."

"They have a dog."

"Yes, of course there's a dog."

"So, basically, a normal family is people who love each other and live anywhere and have a dog."

Becky thought about it. "Yes. That sounds right."

"So, basically, just not your family?"

"Ouch. But yes."

Dakota pulled her into a tight hug that threatened the contents of her mug. "You deserve love, Beck. You deserve all of it."

"Just not with a lawyer or a genius—"

"Nope. Doesn't matter about that. That stuff, that's just the window dressing. Your problem is that you're too worried about the window dressing: the job, the house, the boringness. As your best friend and surrogate sister, I should have steered you right."

"You tried. And you were right when Foster was just a lumberjack."

"I was. God, I thought I was never wrong about love."

"I'm disappointing people all over today."

Dakota sat back and took Becky's face in her hands. "I'm going to allow this pity party for twenty-four hours only. Starting twelve hours ago. Then

Bullhorn's going to get us drunk and we're going to brainstorm ideas for a fundraiser for the shelter."

"To pay for the damage?"

"No, Maddie's parents paid for the damage she did. But the whole thing did make it apparent that I can't put off certain improvements any longer, so I need money."

"God, I'm sorry. I'm sitting here crying over my sad love life . . ."

"Nope. No apologizing. You have half a day yet to wallow."

Becky sighed and leaned against Dakota's shoulder. "Thanks."

"Good. Let's drink."

"Madison, open the door."

"I hate you."

Foster sighed. That was the sixth time she'd said that. Being an older brother was so fun.

He didn't want to do it, but he really needed to talk to his kid sister. "I have Starr with me."

There was a pause. She didn't open the door, but she didn't say she hated him.

"Prove it."

"Starr, give us a little bark, baby." Starr stared at him from her perch on his shoulder. "Starr, attack!" She blinked. "You're just going to have to trust me," he told the door.

"Yeah right. Like I'm ever trusting you again."

"That's not fair . . ." he started, but he didn't want

to have this conversation through a closed door, especially not when his mother was hovering at the end of the hallway. He put Starr down. She jumped up and pawed at his knees. He ignored her. She pawed some more. He didn't pick her up. She barked.

The door opened.

"Hi, Starr, my baby!" Madison scooped a delighted Starr into her arms and snuffled her face into her fur. Foster got a boot in the door before she could slam it in his face. That was all he needed, for her to take the dog hostage.

"Sit down," he said, pointing to the bed. He shut the door behind her and pulled out her desk chair.

"Are you gonna give me a lecture, too, about what a disappointment I am?"

"Madison, you got stoned and destroyed an animal shelter. I'm not disappointed. I'm pissed. What the hell were you thinking?"

"Nothing! I didn't mean to make such a mess. And it's not *destroyed*. God. You're so dramatic."

Foster dropped his head into his hands to keep himself from launching across the room and wringing her neck. He didn't want to traumatize his dog with physical violence. "Madison," he said to the carpet. "Are you listening to yourself?"

She didn't say anything. He looked up and she had her head buried in Starr's back. Starr looked like she was about to fall asleep.

"Madison. Look at me."

"Why? So you can yell at me?" She looked up, though, and she had tears streaming down her face.

"Madison, knock it off. You're not going to cry your way out of this."

She sniffled. He didn't look away. "You're an asshole."

"Language."

"You know what, fuck you. Fuck you and your stupid *language* and your coming in here and telling me what to do like you're the boss of me. You don't know me. You moved to New York with your big fancy life and you think you can just come back here when it's convenient for you and save the day? You're the perfect son, you win all the trophies, and now you're even going to get down on my level to save me from my own shit. And fuck you, I can curse if I want to!"

Foster was pretty sure she was crying for real this time. Her face was ugly and red and there were tears but also snot. He hadn't seen her cry like this since she was a baby. It scared him then, that a little thing could freak out so badly. It was easier to avoid her than it was to keep her from feeling such hurt.

Huh. Insight.

He sat down next to her on the bed and put his arms around her and Starr. She pushed him away at first, but he was stronger, and soon she melted into him, covering his shirt with her real angry, frustrated, confused tears. "I love you, kid," he said into her hair.

"No, you don't." She didn't sound like she wanted to argue about it. She just sounded sad.

"Hey." He tilted her head back and went to wipe her tears away. Then he had second thoughts about that and reached over to her nightstand for a tissue. "I do love you."

"But you wish I was better. Quiet, like Mom, or smarter, like you."

"No. I wish you would think about things before you did them, but I wouldn't change you. Not for a million *me*s."

"Shut up," she said, but he was pretty sure he saw a smile in there.

"You gotta knock it off with the drinking."

"It was just one stupid night. I won't get that crazy again."

"It wasn't one stupid night. You got arrested; that was your stupid night. This was your second stupid night—that I know of. How many other stupid nights are there where you didn't get caught?"

She didn't say anything.

"Do I really have to explain to you how bad it was Saturday night? You or one of your friends could have been seriously hurt."

"Not all shelter dogs are dangerous—"

"No, but when you've got a bunch of crazy people acting erratic around them . . . you probably freaked them out. You were really lucky that one of them didn't react badly. Come on, Madison, you know more about dogs than I do. You knew it was dangerous."

She closed her eyes. "I knew."

"Why did you do it?"

"I don't know." Tears started streaming down her cheeks again. He let her cry. "I just . . . we had a few drinks and we wanted a place to smoke up, and Dylan had been giving me shit for spending so much time at the shelter even when my community service was up, so I wanted to show her what a cool place it was. Jesus, I know it was dumb. You don't have to keep telling me!" She launched herself off the bed, Starr in tow, and started pacing in front of him.

"I don't know why I did it, okay? It didn't even seem like a very good idea at the time. I just couldn't stop myself from saying it, and then I couldn't stop Dylan and all of them from going. And once I was there and we smoked, it was fun, so I thought it wasn't so terrible because we were having fun."

She sat down on her desk chair. "I couldn't help it."

He wanted to absolve her. He wanted to reassure her that all of this was just part of growing up, making mistakes and learning from them. But this felt like more than that.

"Maddie, I love you."

"I know."

"I can't help you."

She sighed. "I know."

"You gotta talk this out with someone who can."

"Like therapy? No, thanks."

"Well, it's gotta be someone who's smarter than me. And someone who's not our parents."

She didn't say anything for a while, just scratched a rhythmic path on Starr's belly. "Fine," she eventually said quietly.

"C'mere," he said, and he stood up and pulled her into his arms. "I'm proud of you."

"I'm not," she said into his chest. "God, I screwed up. Dakota must hate me."

"She might. But she's not going to press charges."

"She should."

"I know she should. But she refuses to."

"Becky must think I'm a total screwup."

"That's possible."

"Can you . . . will you apologize to her for me?"

"Sure . . ." If Becky would ever speak to him again.

"Oh no; she didn't break up with you because of me, did she?"

"No, no, we didn't break up." He didn't think. "We're just . . . she's giving me space."

"Why?"

Because he'd called her emotionally incompetent. "We just . . . are."

She stepped out of his hug. "What did you do?"

"I didn't do anything!" Sort of. "She wants some space, and because we have to work together, I'm going to give it to her."

"What? You're breaking up with her because of work?"

"We're not breaking up!"

"Then why are you letting her get away?"

"I'm not *letting* her do anything. She's a grown-up; she decided she needed space. Besides, her sister is involved in that big case I'm working on, so it's better if we don't spend much time together."

Madison's face twisted in disgust. "You broke up with her because of the case?"

"Again, not broken up. And it's not *because* of the

case. Librarians aren't directly involved in litigation, so it wouldn't technically be a conflict of interest for us to continue to see each other, but I just think it won't look great, so this is for the best."

"Oh my God."

Foster felt the back of his neck to see if he had sprouted a second head. Nope, Madison was just looking at him as if he had.

"You're Dad."

"What? What? No." A second head would be preferable.

"All you care about is your damn case."

"That's not true. I care about Becky; I'm just respecting her wishes. The fact that it coincides with what's best for the case is convenient, yes, but it's not the reason I'm giving her the space she asked for."

"You really believe that, don't you?"

"Madison, I hardly think you're in a position to lecture me—"

"You know what? Fuck you all over again. You *are* just like Dad. Blah, blah, work blinders. At least all Dad does is make sure rich people's money goes to the right places when they die. What does your work even do for humanity?"

"Not everything has to do with humanity."

"No, it has to do with whether you're being challenged and whether you can win. It's not a victory if it's not a fight, right? God, you are so Dad."

He pulled at his collar. He had an uncomfortable feeling Madison was starting to make sense.

"What's your *point*, Foster? What's the point of

winning just to win? I never got that. What are you even winning?"

"First of all—"

"No. Uh-uh. I'm not going to sit here and listen to a list of all the reasons you've come up with to justify your shittiness."

"I am *not* shitty."

"You're a shitty boyfriend."

"She offered me space! I took it!"

Madison just rolled her eyes at him. "You don't deserve this dog."

"You're not keeping Starr."

"What about when you go back to New York, huh? Wasn't that the plan, to win your big case and move on? What was it you said to Dad? Leverage?"

He scratched Starr's ears. "New York. I don't know about that anymore."

"Really?"

"Don't get excited. I'm just . . . keeping my options open." Becky wasn't in New York. He didn't think she'd want to be either. He'd ask her, though. When they were done with their space.

"If you go to New York, you're going to turn into Dad."

"I thought you said I already was."

"There's still hope. I can see it. You just have to get your head out of your ass long enough to realize that you let a great woman go so you could win a case."

"I didn't let her go. It's just a break! And it was her idea!"

"God, you're stupid."

"Explain it to me, then, if you're so smart."

"You're putting your client first. A gigantic, evil corporation named Goliath, which is, like, not even pretending not to be evil."

"First of all, they aren't evil. Secondly, you're oversimplifying it."

"You and Becky are on a break so you can finish your dumb case. Is that it?"

He thought about it. "Aside from the dumb part, yes."

Madison smacked him on the shoulder.

"What was that for?"

"Because it's just like I said. You're putting your job first! That is such a Dad thing! When I was upset that he missed my recitals and games because of work, didn't you tell me not to take it personally, that it was his messed-up logic?"

He did remember saying that to her. But she'd get so upset and he had to make her feel better. The only way he could think to do it was to acknowledge that, yes, their father was a workaholic, but that didn't mean he didn't love her. It just meant that his priorities were whack.

Oh. Now he got it.

Damn, he didn't like being wrong.

"What do you like about Becky?"

Foster sighed. "Madison, this isn't a matter of whether I like her—"

"Indulge me. I'm damaged."

He took a deep breath. Yup, he was getting into this with his kid sister.

"She's . . . she's Becky, you know? You like her, too."

"Yes, but I'm fairly confident I like her for different

reasons than you do. Unless you don't, in which case, you need to work on your game, big brother."

"No, we're . . . we're compatible. In that way."

"In a sex way?"

"Jesus, Madison."

"Well! If you're not going to tell me, I'll make it up. It's because she's hot and blond . . ."

"No, I don't care about that. I did," he said when he saw Madison's eyebrows hit the ceiling. "I mean, I enjoy that about her, but that's not *why* I like her."

"Good. Go on."

"It's . . . I don't know, she's just great. She makes me laugh and she gets me and she makes me feel . . ."

He trailed off. He didn't really want to get into all that with anyone, let alone his kid sister.

"Everything you just said has to do with how she makes you feel. What do you like about *her*?"

"Since when did you become a relationship expert?"

"When I'm grounded, I read a lot. Sue me."

"Maybe I will."

"Shut up. What do you *like* about *her*?"

He closed his eyes. It was the only way he'd be able to say this stuff, by pretending he was alone in the room. That wasn't weird, was it? "I like her because she has the biggest heart of anyone I've ever met. She looks at the world in a way that's not naïve—she's not dumb or anything— but that's just . . . I don't know, optimistic? Like she doesn't think the world is out to get her, that every- thing's a competition."

"So she's nothing like you."

"I also like her because she's funny and because she can see the joy in things. And because she's curious. She wants to get at the heart of people, find out what makes them tick. She has this ability to see underneath all the layers. All my layers. And . . . a bunch of stuff I'm not going to tell you about."

"Thank you. What else?"

"I don't know what else. Everything else. I just know that when she walks into a room, my heart . . ." He put his hand over his heart. He could feel it. It was doing it now, that thing that it did when he saw Becky. "I love her."

He sat there for a minute and let that sink in. He felt his heart beating hard against his hand, and he remembered that last time when he woke up in the middle of the night—before all the crap went down at the shelter—and Becky was listening to his heart because she said it soothed her when she couldn't sleep. And why shouldn't she listen to it? It was hers.

Then he heard sniffling. He opened his eyes and Madison was crying. "Are you crying?" he asked.

"No, shut up," she said and threw another pillow at him. "So now what are you going to do?"

"You're the relationship expert. What should I do?"

"Hmm. Something big, something that shows how much you care."

"She doesn't like being the center of attention."

"She doesn't have to be. Wait, hold on. I've got it."

Chapter Twenty-Four

It was a rough morning. Becky felt like she had a giant hangover, which was weird because she hadn't had anything to drink except tea.

No, wait. That wasn't true. She and Dakota had wallowed in front of bad TV while Bullhorn plied them with drinks until he had to go to work. They vegged and drank and agreed that they would never get lip injections until Bullhorn came home at three in the morning with ice cream.

So she did have a reason to feel bad, and that reason was ice cream and beer and Dakota's lumpy couch. Also, because once Dakota and Bullhorn went to bed, she'd cried out every ounce of moisture in the county. She didn't remember the last time she'd cried so hard. Probably never. Probably because nothing had hurt like this.

She knew her wallowing period was over, but Dakota wasn't up yet, so she gave herself another minute. Because it still hurt. She understood, rationally, the reasons why Foster had pulled away. She'd practically laid the reasons out for him. She just couldn't seem to convince her stupid heart of that.

She should find another job. She didn't want to go back to work to face Foster again. And she didn't really feel that attached to her job anyway. She liked being a librarian, but suddenly she didn't want to work at a place like P&G, where she never knew the details of the cases she was working on. It made her feel like she wasn't really involved. And, yeah, that fact would probably work in her favor if she wanted to fight for her job, but the fact that she didn't even know her own sister was being sued by Goliath . . . and that P&G was defending clients who sued people who were just trying not to kill all the bees. That didn't sit right with her. That made her wonder what else she'd helped P&G take down. What if she was letting people kill polar bears?

But it wasn't her conscience that hurt her the most, although she thought that feeding that guilt might be a good way to keep her mind off the fact that Foster had totally broken her heart.

Nope. Too late.

Of course he wouldn't want to jeopardize his case. And of course he wouldn't want her involved in his family drama. And he was under a lot of stress. The two things he'd moved back to Colorado for had just blown up in his face at once. But this case was about more than just geography. She might not have been on the big-shot attorney fast track, but she knew how it worked. She knew you didn't move from New York to Denver for just any old case. You moved because you were going to be partner. And if he lost this case, there was no way.

So yeah, she got why he was willing to stay away. But it still hurt that he'd jumped at the opportunity so quickly.

And the worst part was, she wasn't going to get to see Starr anymore. Just when they were starting to become friends.

"Hey, how'd you sleep?" Dakota came down the stairs in baggy pants and her bathrobe, rubbing her eyes. Becky quickly shoved her face in the pillow.

"Oh no. Are you still crying? Hey, I told you, your pity party time is up." She sounded harsh, but she sat down on the couch and rubbed Becky's back anyway.

"It's not about that. It's that . . . I just realized I won't get to see Starr anymore. I love that dog!"

"Oh, sweetheart." Dakota wrapped her in a full hug. "I know you do. Maybe we can arrange some visitations or something. We'll work it out."

Becky sat up and wiped her eyes. "It's fine. I mean, yes, let's think about that, but for now, it's fine. It's done. We're done."

"Are you sure? He called Bullhorn like twelve times last night."

"He did?"

"Yeah. Bullhorn finally picked up, and he said he couldn't get through to you."

"Oh. My phone probably died. Like everything in my life."

"That's the spirit. Come on, bring that dead phone

into the kitchen. My charger is in there, and you can make me coffee while I solve all your problems."

Dakota held out her hand to help Becky up off the couch.

"Wait a second." Becky took Dakota's left hand and flipped it over. "What's this?"

"Oh, that." Dakota took her hand back and fiddled with the ring on her finger. "I didn't want to tell you until you were feeling better."

"Bullhorn?"

"No, the other man who's been sleeping in my bed for the past few months."

"Dakota! I'm so happy for you!" Love may be an unreachable goal for her, but she wasn't a total monster. She squeezed her best friend into a tight hug. "When did he ask you?"

"Last night when he got home."

"While I was on the couch sobbing? How romantic."

"He checked to make sure you were asleep. He said he was going to wait until we went camping next weekend, but with the stuff with you and Foster . . ."

"I got nervous that she'd escape my clutches."

Bullhorn came down the stairs, his hair sticking up at crazy angles, and he scooped Dakota up around the waist and spun her around.

"Never," Dakota said. He put her down, slowly, and they started kissing.

Which was Becky's cue to find Dakota's charger in the kitchen. And she'd make coffee for the love-birds, too.

While the coffee brewed, she turned on her phone. No new messages. She wasn't disappointed, she told herself. She'd given him space; he was taking the space. Besides, her pity party was over.

"Hey, what about this fundraiser?" she called out to the living room.

"Oh that." Dakota walked into the kitchen, Bull-horn trailing behind with his arms around her waist. "Um . . . I think we've got that taken care of."

Becky looked at the clock. "That was fast."

"Something came up. It's still tentative, but it's promising."

"OK. What can I do?"

"Nothing. I mean, show up."

"You do realize that less than twelve hours ago you told me you required me to help you brain-storm."

"I had a productive morning."

"You got engaged and you planned a fundraiser."

"Hey, I'm efficient."

"Should I at least bring my camera?"

"Yes. Definitely bring your camera."

Chapter Twenty-Five

Becky didn't feel like going to a party.

She reminded herself it wasn't a party; it was a fundraiser for the shelter, which was a good cause she very much supported. And she was technically working at it because Dakota wanted her to be the photographer.

Well, Dakota had told her to "carry her camera," but Becky understood what she meant.

Besides, it would be good to hide behind the camera. She didn't think Foster would be there—surely Dakota wouldn't welcome him or any reminder of that crappy night—but she'd also spent the week studiously avoiding him, and she didn't want to take any chances.

She was giving him space.

And she was looking for a new job.

It turned out she had a reputation in Denver, and when she finally worked up the courage to call a recruiter, she'd gotten all kinds of interest. She just had to decide what direction she wanted to go in.

Not another P&G; she was still sure about that. But something where she could do some good.

That was for later. For now, she was going to a party.

It felt weird wearing a dress to the shelter, and she was pretty sure she'd regret it once the first set of muddy paws came out, but Dakota had insisted.

She finally found a parking spot halfway down the block. The lot was full and she barely squeezed into the spot she'd found. As she climbed up the long driveway—flanked on either side by parked cars—she heard the sounds of a live band and the shouts of kids. So, not the stuffy kind of fundraiser. Good thing Dakota was specific in her dress code instructions: cute, but not stuffy, and definitely a dress.

She smoothed down the front of her sundress and buttoned one of the buttons on her cardigan. It wasn't quite warm enough for it, but it was sunny, and she figured if she got cold, she could just run some laps with one of the hounds. Maybe that would inspire one of these families to take a dog home with them.

There was a big banner across the front of the shelter that read "New Hope Family Day." There were tables set up with games and crafts, and people were milling around, enjoying the sunshine and the barbecue.

There was even a kissing booth. She pulled off her lens cap. It was too cute. A dog who looked a lot like Rizzo was manning it, delighting kids with slobbery kisses as their parents deposited cash in the nearby jar.

She got closer to get a good angle. The dog barked at her and tried to climb out of the booth.

"Rizzo, stay!" A woman standing behind the booth held on to Rizzo's leash as the dog vibrated with excitement. But she stayed.

"This is Rizzo?" Becky asked her. "I thought she looked familiar. What is she doing back here?"

"It's not what you think," the woman assured her. "She's mine. She's just volunteering for today. Part of the New Hope Family."

"Got it. It's good to see you, Rizzie." She gave Rizzo's haunches a vigorous rub.

"Say, are you Becky?" the woman asked.

"Yes," she said, straightening up from molesting the woman's dog.

"You take the photos for the web site, right? I'm Kelly. Thank you so much for doing that. I fell in love with Rizzo from that picture."

"Oh, thanks. Wow, that's really nice to hear."

"I don't suppose you'd consider selling me a higher-res copy? So I can get it framed?"

"Oh, sure. I hadn't thought about that. I mean, just make a donation to the shelter and I'll be sure you get it, does that sound OK?"

"Perfect. Hey, Brian!" Kelly called out to a man working the barbecue station. "This is Becky!"

"Becky!" He handed off his tongs and came over and enveloped Becky in a hug.

"OK. Great. Hugging strangers."

"Sorry," Brian said. "I can't tell you how grateful I am to all of you. I adopted Tigger."

"Oh! Bouncy Tigger! How's he doing?"

"He's perfect. My wife has PTSD and he never leaves her side. I never would have found him if it wasn't for your picture."

"Oh, I don't know about that."

Brian hugged her again. "Thank you."

As soon as she disentangled herself from Brian—and wiped away a few happy tears—she went in search of Dakota. It took longer than she expected, though, because she kept getting waylaid by people who had adopted dogs from New Hope based on pictures she had taken.

It was enough to make a girl's head swell up.

But then she saw Foster.

Which brought her crashing right down to Earth.

He was looking gorgeous and scruffy and he was carrying Starr, who was sporting a festive floral bandanna. It kind of matched the pattern of her dress.

Great. Just what she needed. She'd offered to give him space and now she was dressed like his dog.

Before she could escape back into the fray, he spotted her and made a beeline right to her.

"Hey," he said. He leaned in to kiss her on the cheek. He was smiling like a goofball.

Didn't this guy know that he'd broken her heart?

"Starr missed you," he said and dumped the dog into her arms.

"Oh," she said, instantly melting. "I missed you, too, sweetheart."

"So. Ah. How are you?"

"Great. Fine. This is a nice party."

"Yup. Haven't seen you around the office much."

"Oh." Wasn't that the point of space? "I've been busy." Looking for other jobs. To give herself some space.

Being near him just reinforced her determination to get away from P&G. He smelled good. She wanted to lick him.

Not really part of their current deal.

"How're you?" she asked, even though she could have answered that just by looking at him. Happy. Hot.

God, why did he have to have that stupid beard back?

"Fine, great. Working a lot."

"I bet."

"I'm writing up a settlement deal for Goliath."

"A settlement? I thought you guys were going to win big?"

He shrugged. "This was the best way. We came to terms on Friday, so I was there all last night working."

"Bummer."

"I would have called you."

"But you were working."

"I wanted to be done first. Get that out of the way."

"Sure. Take care of the client first, I get it."

"No, that's not . . . can we go somewhere to talk?"

That sounded very dangerous, with him looking so sexy and earnest and her wearing a dress and remembering all the creative ways he had of getting into her pants.

"How's Maddie?" she asked, because that was the only way she could think of tamping down some of the rampant sexual energy she couldn't seem to stop sending his way.

"She's good, I think."

"You think?"

"She's, uh. She's away. At a program."

"A program? Like rehab?"

"Yeah. It's a program for teenage girls. They're on a ranch in Wyoming. She left on Wednesday."

"Wow. That's a change."

"Yeah. I'm pretty sure she still hates me for it. Especially when she found out she'd be missing this party."

"Dakota was going to let her come?"

"I didn't ask."

"Smart. Well, I hope she does well there. A ranch? Is she a horse person?"

"She was obsessed when she was a kid, but I don't know. She's not a kid anymore."

"No, she's not."

"But the horses let my parents tell their friends that she's on a vacation instead of at a program for troubled teens."

"Well, as long as Maddie gets the help she needs, right?"

"Right. Hey, listen, I'm really sorry . . ."

Those were the words she'd wanted to hear from

him. She hadn't realized how badly she'd wanted to hear them until he said them.

But then she was tackled by a flying Dakota, who whisked her off to meet more pet parents who'd fallen in love via her photos.

She wanted to take new photos. She would have, if she wasn't still holding Starr.

"I saw you talking to Foster," Dakota whispered to her between dog families. "What did he say?"

"Well, he started to apologize, but then you Tasmanian deviled me."

"Oh, whoops. I promised him I would give him time. I just couldn't wait anymore. Look at all these happy people with their happy dogs!"

"Wait, what do you mean, you promised him? I thought you hated him."

"I do. I did. Then he got this great idea for a fundraiser . . ."

"This was his idea?"

"This wasn't just his idea. This was all his doing. Well, him and his mother." Dakota waved, and Becky followed her gaze to where Lydia Deacon was standing behind a table, selling New Hope T-shirts and Frisbees. "Smile at her. I want to stay on her good side."

Becky smiled. "Why would my smiling have anything to do with that?"

Dakota stopped smiling and waving and looked right at Becky. "Didn't Foster tell you?"

"Tell me what? Dakota, what's going on here?"

"This whole party is for you."

"What? No, it isn't. It's a fundraiser."

"Yes, well, it's conveniently disguised as a fundraiser from which I'll reap all the benefits, but that's just a cover. Beck, he did all this for you."

She looked over to where Foster was standing with Bullhorn, who was trying to disentangle what looked like half a dozen leashes attached to half a dozen hyper dogs.

Foster caught her eye and started toward her.

She froze.

"Hi," he said.

"We already did that."

"Oh, right." He ran his hand through his hair. Was he nervous?

"Did you want your dog back?" she asked, and dumped Starr into his arms.

"Thanks."

She watched him settle Starr against his shoulder and tried not to melt. This whole thing was for her?

"So, ah, I don't know what Dakota told you . . ."

"That you threw this party for me but disguised it as a fundraiser."

"That's pretty much it. I didn't think you'd come if you knew it was for you."

They were interrupted by a young couple and their pit bull, who Becky didn't recognize at all until they told her that he used to be called Zero, and then she remembered the shivering little puppy who had to be coaxed out of his cage with bacon treats.

"He's Ulysses now. Thank you so much."

"Do you mind if we go somewhere quieter?" he asked when the couple had gone. "Just for a minute."

"Yes, sure. I'll probably pass out if I blush anymore."

He took her hand and led her to the edge of the lot, where the grass turned to woods, woods that often deposited hungry strays on New Hope's doorstep.

He stopped and faced her, but he didn't let go of her hand. He took a deep breath. Let it out.

Part of her wanted to help him out, let him off the hook for doing what was her idea in the first place. But she decided to be patient and let him say what he wanted to say.

"I love you."

Well. That wasn't what she was expecting.

She looked up at him. Those eyes. That beard. God, she missed him. "What?"

"Sorry, that came out wrong."

"No, I'm pretty sure it came out loud and clear."

"I was supposed to give you a whole speech about how I never should have put the case before you, even though you offered, and I never should have shut you out when Madison needed you. When I needed you. And about how stupid and bullheaded I was being, and about how you make me a better person and I didn't even realize it until you let me push you away and that I miss you so, so much. I was supposed to say all that stuff first."

"Oh. Well, it's not too late. If you want to say it now." She smiled at him. She couldn't help it.

"I love you so much, Becky. And I've been so stupid. And I didn't know how to make it up to you."

"So you threw me a party?"

"Madison said I had to do something big."

"But you disguised it as a fundraiser?"

"I know you hate being the center of attention. I had to figure out a way to make sure you got the praise you deserve. Make sure you knew that, yeah, your family sucks, but people know what you're worth."

"Wow."

"Too much?"

"It's a lot." She looked over at the party. The people, the animals, the noise. It was all for her.

"Will Starr be OK if you put her down for a minute?"

"Sure," he said, and he bent down to deposit Starr on the grass, which she immediately started investigating. "Why?"

"Because I want to kiss you and I don't want to crush your dog."

He wrapped his arms around her. "See? That's what I mean. Always thinking about others."

"I love you."

He beamed at her. "I love you, too. So much. You don't know how much I missed . . ."

He was embarrassing her with all that sweetness. And he was holding her tight, which reminded her how good it felt to be in his arms and close to his heart. And while she loved listening to him wax poetic about all the ways he loved her, she had other things on her mind.

"Hey, Foster," she said, cutting him off.

"Yeah?"

"Shut up and kiss me."

Epilogue

Becky pulled into the driveway and smiled. She did that every time she pulled into her driveway. It was totally sappy, but she couldn't help it. She had a house. It made her happy.

It didn't have a white picket fence, but it did have a fenced-in backyard that Starr enjoyed exploring. She had identified several favorite outdoor napping spots for when she wanted a change from napping on the back of the couch.

Becky still couldn't believe it was hers. She still didn't quite believe it, no matter how much Miranda insisted. Miranda had given her the down payment. Had forced it on her, really. She'd even somehow wired it into her bank account after Becky refused it the first time. Miranda had plenty of money, she insisted. She wasn't going to use it all.

It hadn't led to a traditional sisterly relationship. Miranda still seemed to struggle with how to talk to people when it wasn't about chromosomes or molecules. They were never going to get pedicures or go to brunch or gab about their sex lives. But Becky understood that the money was Miranda's way of showing Becky that she loved her and it still felt weird, but, well, she loved the house.

She unlocked the front door and hip checked it open; it was an old house with all kinds of quirks. "Honey, I'm home!" she shouted, because Foster had mentioned something about working from home today.

Because he was still Foster, and he still worked too much. But now he worked for himself, having set up his own practice that specialized in defending scientists in intellectual property cases. The money wasn't great yet—it would never be Polak & Glass-meyer money—but he was making enough now that his pride didn't hurt so badly, living in a house that his girlfriend's sister bought them.

She heard him in the kitchen, singing badly to the radio. She stopped by the couch to give Starr a scratch behind the ears, then followed her nose and her ears to see what her man was up to.

He was cooking. The smells could have told her that. They couldn't, however, have told her that he'd be standing in front of the stove, stirring a pan wearing an apron.

And nothing else.

"You're early!"

"You're naked!"

"I wanted to surprise you."

"Well, I'm definitely surprised. What is all this?"

The table was set, there were flowers in a vase, and her boyfriend was at the stove, naked.

He pulled her toward him and kissed her hello. She may have reached down to enjoy his nakedness a little. He may have growled into her mouth.

"It's been a year and a half," he said when they came up for air.

"A year and a half?"

"A year and a half since you picked me up from that crappy sports bar and ravaged me."

"I remember it being a pretty mutual ravaging."

He kissed her again. "We didn't get to celebrate one year because of Dakota and Bullhorn's wedding, so I thought . . ." He hoisted her up on the counter.

"You thought you'd surprise me with naked dinner?" She wrapped her arms around his shoulders and pulled him closer.

"That was the idea."

She tilted up her head and he kissed her again. His mouth moved down her neck, kissing a path while his hands worked on the buttons of her blouse.

"Why didn't you finish cooking, then get naked?"

He stopped kissing. "Hmm. I see your point."

She smiled, but she didn't say anything. She loved it when he admitted she was right. It was almost as sexy as his butt.

And then he went back to her neck and her buttons, and she forgot all about being right.

"You're very sweet," she said softly. He kissed her and started to pull her blouse off her shoulders while she shivered.

Then the front door opened.

Then Maddie screamed.

"What are you guys doing?"

"You're supposed to be at a barbecue!" Foster shouted back at her as he tried to cover both Becky and his nakedness.

Maddie was living with them for her senior year, under the condition that she follow their rules. The summer had been great, and Maddie was celebrating at a last-day-of-summer barbecue at a friend's house—a friend with parents who had a strict no-controlled-substances rule and who would be present the entire time.

But she wasn't. She was standing behind the front door she had just slammed while Becky buttoned her shirt and Foster ran into their room for a pair of shorts.

Starr let out a halfhearted bark from the couch.

"It's OK now," Becky called once Foster was dressed.

Maddie peeked her head around the door. "Are you sure?"

"No, we're playing a hilarious joke where you see me naked," Foster said. "Come inside. Why aren't you at the party?"

"I had to stop by the shelter."

Once Maddie had finished her horse-farm rehab, as she called it, she'd begged Dakota to let her volunteer at the shelter again. Dakota had refused, but she'd hired her as a part-time animal technician with the understanding that any hint of funny business would result in her being banned for life.

"Big payday?" Foster asked as he walked toward the door to usher his sister inside.

"Sort of."

"What the hell is that?"

Maddie came in, followed by an absolutely enormous dog on a leash.

"It's a dog," she said helpfully.

"Are you sure? It looks like a horse."

"It's an Irish wolfhound."

Starr hopped off the couch and came over to investigate. Becky held her breath—Starr wasn't great with other dogs—but the giant horse-dog bent her head down and let Starr sniff her nose and it seemed fine.

"Her name is Rosie," Maddie explained. "She came in as a stray yesterday. The vet says she's around six years old, which is pretty old for a girl like her."

"That's great, but what is she doing in our house?"

"Well, they don't really have a big enough cage for her at the shelter, and Dakota was trying to find a foster . . ."

Starr barked once, then trotted over to the couch. She got halfway, then turned around and barked again. Rosie lumbered after her.

Becky watched as Starr hopped up on the back of the couch and barked again. Rosie sniffed the cushions—which were shorter than she was—and climbed on. Starr walked in a circle and curled up with a sigh. Rosie put her head on the arm of the couch and sighed.

Becky put her arm around Foster's waist. He was staring in a daze at the canine takeover of their living room, but he put his arm around her shoulders anyway. "They seem to get along," she said.

"It's just fostering," Maddie said hopefully.

"As long as it's only temporary," he said, and despite Maddie's protestations, Becky leaned up and gave Foster a big ol' kiss.

Praise for *The Undateable*

"Represents the best of a new kind of contemporary romance: socially aware and laugh-out-loud funny, with a love story that's real enough to imagine reading about on Twitter."
—*Kirkus Reviews*, starred review

"Funny, engrossing, and delightfully written."
—*Publishers Weekly*, starred review

Dear Maria,

I'm about to graduate from college and I think my boyfriend is going to propose. My parents really like him, but they say we're too young to get married. I really want to start a family, and I love him so much! We've been through everything together. We lost our virginities to each other. We've been talking about what we'll do after graduation, but he's never brought up marriage.

If he asks, should I say yes?

Distressed About Saying Yes in Alamo Square

Dear Distressed,

You are so young. I can barely remember what it was like to be that young, except that marriage was the last thing on my mind. Marriage is a lifelong commitment, and who knows what will happen when you get out in the real world? You might discover that the path you set yourself on is not the path you were meant to be on. Your boyfriend might find the same thing. Hell, you might want to have sex with other people!

Think about that. He is the only person you'll have sex with for the rest of your life. Unless you have an open marriage, which is definitely something you should bring up before he asks.

Imagine your perfect life together. Imagine what your house will look like, how many kids you'll have, what your career will be. Nice, right? Now imagine that none of that happens. You have a dead-end job that you took just to pay the bills. You can barely afford the kids you have, or maybe you find out you can't have kids. You live in the Bay Area, so guess what, you can't afford a house. Life sucks. Is your boyfriend still the person you want to be with?

I can't tell you what to do, Distressed, but if I could, I would tell you: when he asks, say, "Hell no."

Kisses,
Maria

It was seventeen past one and Bernie was hangry. She thought longingly of her midmorning banana, abandoned and lonely on her kitchen counter, and of her leftover lentil soup, waiting patiently in the insulated bag under her desk. All her food was so far away. And even if it was right in front of her, she wouldn't eat at the information desk. It would set a bad example. She had enough trouble keeping her student workers off their cell phones while they were on the desk; she didn't need them eating, too.

She looked at the clock again. Eighteen after one. Carly was a wonderful employee in many ways; she was friendly and she seemed unflappable in the face of panicked procrastinators. She had ended up in the library as her work-study assignment, but after four years, she was now considering library school. Bernie was glad. She'd be a great librarian.

A late librarian, but a great one.

As if Bernie's rising hunger-induced annoyance conjured her, Carly came sprinting through the lobby, slowing down to a power walk once she crossed the threshold of the library. She mouthed a wincing apology to Bernie, who just shrugged. She could write her up, but Carly was a senior. She'd be graduating in a few months, and anyway, Bernie was about to eat lunch so she didn't really care.

"I'm so sorry." Carly was breathless when she finally reached the desk. She dropped her heavy shoulder bag on the floor next to the reference computer. "Evan was . . ." She blushed, then stopped. Bernie was grateful. She'd learned way too much about Carly's personal life, and the oversharing had only multiplied since Carly had started dating Evan. Evan was a musical theater major—not gay— and they were supposed to be saving themselves for marriage. Bernie ignored the alarm bells and minded her own business, or as much as Carly would let her mind her own business. For example, a few weeks into the new semester, Carly was floating around and more tardy than usual, and when Bernie asked her what was up, she got a long, metaphor-filled description of Carly's deflowering by the not-gay—and apparently not-waiting-for-marriage—Evan.

It was sweet, Bernie reminded herself. Young love and all that. She had been young and foolish and in love before. Carly would grow out of it, just as surely as Bernie had.

That was depressing, she thought.

Which was surely just the hunger talking.

"There's nothing carrying over," Bernie explained, her mind half on her lunch. In addition to soup, there was also a cupcake. She had forgotten all about the cupcake. Her stomach growled. "It's art history time again," she said, referring to the annual Intro to Art History term paper rush they got this time in the semester. "I pulled a few of the books this morning"—she pointed to a small cart of giant art books near the desk—"so if you could check the links on the web site, make sure they're all still good . . ."

Bernie was distracted by a big crowd of students entering the library. Her heart sank even as her public-service smile lit up. She couldn't leave Carly to handle this many students by herself. Carly was unflappable, but Bernie wasn't a sadist.

"Hi, can I help—"

Bernie started to greet them, thinking they'd all come over from a class together and maybe they wanted a tour. Bernie didn't have any tours on her calendar, but that never stopped a professor from sending a group over. But then they all stopped just shy of the desk and turned their backs to her. Were they protesting? Who would protest the library? Then she heard music coming from the back of the Student Blob, and she was just about to launch into her autopilot Please-Use-Headphones, when the Blob started to shake.

Oh my God, she thought. *They're dancing*.

She looked at Carly, as if the young person might have some explanation for the Undulating Student Blob—was this a thing the kids were doing, Bernie wondered while reminding herself that she was only thirty-one, still a kid, maybe. Carly, however, looked like she was on the amused end of the bemused spectrum. *Kids*, Bernie thought. Then: *I am very, very hungry*.

Then the lyrics started, and Bernie recognized the pop song—something about love forever and crap like that. But her old person brain remembered that it was sung by a woman, and this was not a woman singing. The dancing blob parted and there, like a singing Moses, was Evan. He was holding a small microphone plugged into his cell phone, karaoking over the original song. As he sang and the music crescendoed, the dancers moved in a joyful, if not totally coordinated, circle around the information desk. Bernie watched them swish and swirl around, wondering where they were going to go next. She started to say something to Carly, but Carly was not watching the dancers. She was watching Evan, who had swirled up to her and *onto* the desk. He was dancing on the information desk. That was not allowed. Bernie should stop him.

Then a couple of the burlier dancers were behind the desk—another thing Bernie should stop—and they lifted Carly, who squealed but took Evan's hand as he led her in a few complicated but clearly familiar moves on the desk.

Two people dancing on the information desk. Bernie definitely should not just stand there with her mouth open.

Then the dancing stopped, and so did Evan's singing, although the music continued in the background. Bernie remembered this part. This was the part where the singer talked to the singee about how much she loved him and there were some metaphors about sunshine and butterflies. But Evan wasn't metaphorizing. He was getting down on one knee. Then he was reaching into his pocket. Then, accompanied by the sound of dozens of undergraduate cell phones taking pictures, he pulled open a small square box.

"Carly Monica Hilbert, you have made me the happiest man in the world. Will you make me even happier by becoming my wife?"

No, no, no, thought Bernie. This isn't right. They are way too young. They just started drinking legally—they couldn't possibly be ready to get married!

But Carly wasn't listening to Bernie's silent objections. She wasn't looking to her mentor for advice or approval. She was just looking at Evan, her eyes shining, and she nodded.

There was a surge from the crowd as Evan stood and twirled Carly in his arms, then shakily put the ring on her finger.

Bernie was never going to get to eat lunch.

FALLING FOR TROUBLE

The riot grrrl and the bookworm—just the pair to get the whole town talking . . .

Liam Byrd loves Halikarnassus, New York.
He loves its friendliness, its nosiness,
the vibrant library at the center of it all.
And now that Joanna Green is home,
the whole town sizzles. A rebel like her stirs up
excitement, action, desire—at least in Liam.

Joanna never thought she'd have to come back to
her dull, tiny fishbowl of a hometown ever again.
She almost had a record deal for her all-girl rock
band. She almost had it made in L.A.
And then her deal went sour and her granny
broke her leg . . . and now here she is, running
into everybody's favorite librarian every time she
heads to a dive bar or catches up with old friends.

He has charm, he has good taste in music—and
the sight of him in running shorts is dangerously
distracting. But when he loves her old town and
she can't wait to check out, their new romance is
surely destined for the book drop. . . .

"Jo? Joey Green?"

And that, in one frustrating nickname, was the reason why Joanna Green never came back to Halikarnassus. The fact that it was a nosy little town with one bar and few people worth drinking with, she could deal with. It was more the fact that everyone in town seemed obsessed with the Joanna she had been in high school—a screwup and a hell-raiser and a general bad influence. She hadn't been home in years, and that one nickname made it abundantly clear that no one was going to try to get to know Joanna the Adult.

Not that Joanna the Adult was any less of a screwup. Hell, that was why she was standing in the airport, waiting in baggage claim for the suitcase holding all her worldly possessions—with the exception of her guitar, which she would never, in a million years, trust to baggage handlers.

Coming home as an abject failure with your tail between your legs was one thing, Joanna thought. Having to explain that failure to a bunch of people who didn't expect anything more from you was a new level of humiliation she wasn't sure she could deal with. *Just keep an eye out for your suitcase,* she told herself. *You don't have to talk to anyone. You just need to grab the bag that's holding all your worldly possessions, convince a cab to take you all the way to Halikarnassus, and hope that Granny is home to lend you cab fare.*

Totally an adult.

"I thought it was you!"

Joanna could no longer ignore the persistent nostalgia at her elbow. A young woman in an enormous gray scarf was looking at her expectantly. Joanna tried to place her . . . she looked vaguely familiar . . .

"Oh my gosh, you don't remember me. Skyler Carrington?" Scarf girl gave her a hopeful look.

"Holy crap, Skyler? I thought you were like . . ." The last time Joanna had seen Skyler, Joanna was getting in big trouble for making her cry because she wouldn't let her play with her very expensive guitar. Skyler had been what, five? Seven? She was ten years younger than Joanna, a fact that had caused Trina, Joanna's best friend and Skyler's big sister, a minor adolescent breakdown. Then, of course, Trina was ruthlessly protective of her sister who was, frankly, a brat.

Skyler had been three. Or five. Or whatever. That was a long time ago. She was probably much better now. And wasn't that why Joanna had avoided coming home? Because she knew people would only see her as she was back then? Pot and black kettle and all that.

Back then, Joanna was a foulmouthed, rebellious, broke teenager. Now she was . . . well, she wasn't a teenager.

God, how depressing. She'd left town to shake off the image everybody had of her only to find that the reason they had that image was because it was who she was.

Except that now she was old. And Skyler Carrington was as tall as she was.

And Skyler Carrington was leaning forward to give Joanna a hug. "Trina's not going to believe this! What are you doing here?"

"Just, uh . . ." Skyler Carrington didn't need to know the whole sad, sordid story, and it made Joanna feel a little better that news of her epic failure hadn't reached Halikarnassus yet. At least, not the airport two hours from Halikarnassus. "Just visiting."

"Granny! How's Granny?"

"Good, fine." She hoped anyway. Granny hadn't answered her early-morning call. But then, ever since Granny retired, she was always busy. Still, she usually returned calls.

Joanna waved her hand. "What are you doing here? Love the scarf."

"Oh my God, I just finished a semester in France. I'm, like, so not used to speaking English! And everyone here is so . . . American!"

"You'll get that, what with being in America," Joanna suggested.

"I'm just having, like, culture shock. Literally

everything in France is, like, so much better. I can't even with this." Skyler waved her hand around.

Joanna couldn't even with the baggage claim either. She also couldn't with this kid having adventures in France while Joanna had been working hard, making music, then throwing it all away in one stupid night. Skyler had probably done more in her teenage life than Joanna had in her . . . more than teenage life. They both talked big; this kid had actually done big things.

Fortunately, the baggage claim started to move and, as if the gods of Joanna's hometown shame were looking down upon her struggle to keep it together in a conversation with her old friend's formerly bratty toddler little sister, her suitcase came out first.

"Well, this is me. Nice to see you."

Skyler reached forward to help Joanna with her suitcase. "Are you going to be home for a while? Trina is going to die when I tell her I saw you."

Joanna pretended not to hear. She just waved and lost herself in the crowd, dragging all of her worldly possessions behind her.

Connect with Us

Visit us online at
KensingtonBooks.com
to read more from your favorite authors, see books
by series, view reading group guides, and more.

Join us on social media

for sneak peeks, chances to win books and prize packs,
and to share your thoughts with other readers.

facebook.com/kensingtonpublishing
twitter.com/kensingtonbooks

Tell us what you think!

To share your thoughts, submit a review,
or sign up for our eNewsletters, please visit:
KensingtonBooks.com/TellUs.

Books by Bestselling Author
Fern Michaels

___**The Jury**	0-8217-7878-1	$6.99US/$9.99CAN
___**Sweet Revenge**	0-8217-7879-X	$6.99US/$9.99CAN
___**Lethal Justice**	0-8217-7880-3	$6.99US/$9.99CAN
___**Free Fall**	0-8217-7881-1	$6.99US/$9.99CAN
___**Fool Me Once**	0-8217-8071-9	$7.99US/$10.99CAN
___**Vegas Rich**	0-8217-8112-X	$7.99US/$10.99CAN
___**Hide and Seek**	1-4201-0184-6	$6.99US/$9.99CAN
___**Hokus Pokus**	1-4201-0185-4	$6.99US/$9.99CAN
___**Fast Track**	1-4201-0186-2	$6.99US/$9.99CAN
___**Collateral Damage**	1-4201-0187-0	$6.99US/$9.99CAN
___**Final Justice**	1-4201-0188-9	$6.99US/$9.99CAN
___**Up Close and Personal**	0-8217-7956-7	$7.99US/$9.99CAN
___**Under the Radar**	1-4201-0683-X	$6.99US/$9.99CAN
___**Razor Sharp**	1-4201-0684-8	$7.99US/$10.99CAN
___**Yesterday**	1-4201-1494-8	$5.99US/$6.99CAN
___**Vanishing Act**	1-4201-0685-6	$7.99US/$10.99CAN
___**Sara's Song**	1-4201-1493-X	$5.99US/$6.99CAN
___**Deadly Deals**	1-4201-0686-4	$7.99US/$10.99CAN
___**Game Over**	1-4201-0687-2	$7.99US/$10.99CAN
___**Sins of Omission**	1-4201-1153-1	$7.99US/$10.99CAN
___**Sins of the Flesh**	1-4201-1154-X	$7.99US/$10.99CAN
___**Cross Roads**	1-4201-1192-2	$7.99US/$10.99CAN

Available Wherever Books Are Sold!
Check out our website at www.kensingtonbooks.com